The Secret Diary of a Single Christian Lady

(Volume 2)

... based on true life stories

www.thesecretdiary.net

Albyrims

ISBN: 9789714899742

Published/Printed by:

PatUch Concepts

patuchconcepts@gmail.com

+234 706 898 7100

"The Secret Diary of a Single Christian Lady" initially debuted as "Memoires of a Single Christian Lady" on the Eve Afrique Business and News Facebook page and was subsequently featured on The Trent, known as Nigeria's foremost internet newspaper. This book comprises Ema's personal memoirs, providing readers with a glimpse into her recollections and experiences over time.

To ensure a seamless reading experience, some aspects of time and space have been adjusted. It's important to note that, except for instances involving public figures, any similarities to individuals, living or deceased, are purely coincidental.

Therefore, the author assumes no responsibility for any unintended resemblances in this work to the personal lives of any individuals. This book is brought to you by the creative writers at Irims Starglazzers' desk, offering a unique perspective and storytelling that reflects the diverse experiences of its author, Ema.

Acknowledgment

I want to thank everyone that has made this book possible, especially to all those that read the first volume. They were a big encouragement for the publication of this volume.

I want to first of all thank my mum, three brothers and three sisters for all their support on this journey. You guys are the best. May the Lord bless you all immensely.

I also appreciate all my relatives and friends who chipped in their opinions and perspectives. Thank you all for your support and encouragement.

A big thank you to the EveAfrique online family and all my Facebook friends for reading the memoires when they were posted online; your positive feedback was a huge encouragement, especially for the production of this book.

I want to specially thank Ivy Etokapan for giving me the final nudge and the platform to make these writings public. I also thank Reverend Kester Oshioreame for the constant nudging to go public and ensuring that I had the opportunity to continue utilizing my editing skills.

Above and most important of all, I appreciate and give all the glory to God!

CONTENTS

26

Office Wahala

After a tiring weekend (I had gone to the market and decided to really cook up a storm, enough to last me and any guest I would have for a month – it's been a while since I did that), this morning, the single lady's life filled me with a few smiles and a sense of relief from the minute I got out of bed (which was exactly an hour to office time - I had no kids to make me wake up 5 hours before normal humans should be awake).

I skipped breakfast (which I consider another perk of being single - there's no man and children to ensure I feed before stepping out). I didn't even bother to make up or try hard to look good (after all, there's no husband to impress - I am under no obligation to look attractive if I don't feel like it). Working wives who still go to market and cook must have some extra strength from somewhere o!

Anyway, I was enjoying the thought of my freedom until I got to the office. Every promotion comes with its own problems and I have been facing these problems ever since I was promoted above my colleagues - who by the way I have worked with for almost two years; who by the way felt they and not I deserved the promotion considering they had been employed before me.

There are others who are probably envious of my accomplishments because they always seem happy to add that, '...but she is still single,' when talks about me come up; my promotion just drove them crazy - it's almost as if because one is a single girl she doesn't deserve anything good in life - as if being single must be some sort of punishment for sins committed in a previous life.

They have this knack for referring to me as, 'that small girl' and trying to emphasize my 'singleness' as some sort of major deformity that I have.

Try struggling to find a balance between doing your job as a leader and being cordial towards people who have been your contemporaries for a while, without appearing proud or nasty - a very difficult feat to accomplish. I overheard Kelechi 'Larw' say in a loud whisper when I walked past her into my office;

Kelechi: O! Church! Some people cannot greet again because they have become madam. Who knows what they did to get the promotion? All these single girls, is there anything they can't do for money?

So said the 'husband snatching', 'cohabiting with another person's husband' Kelechi who by the way was appraised the lousiest staff of the year. Kelechi, her shenanigans, her lousy accent and poor work ethics were the least of my problems today anyway.

The new male staff who strutted himself around the office as if he were God's gift to women since Adam, was actually my major problem - not just because he was worse than Kelechi when it came to presentations - being one of the few single males among so many females in the office, he felt entitled to me (I mean relationship-wise) – I am sure it's because of my position in the office.

During his presentation today at a meeting I had worked my head off to organize (a meeting with 3 international organizations that would become our funders if all went well), the new 'male staff' insisted on embarrassing the whole office with his 'American accent.'

Male Staff: The cost of 'transporthation, accredithation and feeding everythay within this stathe'......

I didn't hear anything else beyond that point. I couldn't figure out where he was getting the 'Th' sound from and who told him he could replace the 'T' sound with 'Th'. I could see the confused expression on the faces of our international visitors, especially the British one and I could see my boss glaring at me in anger.

I was almost sure this was a set-up, Kelechi must have briefed this guy, if not why would he insist on disgracing me. Why didn't I think of anyone else to do this presentation – how would I have known that the presence of white people will make him go over-board with his fake 'American accent'?

The fellow had the nerve to wink at me when he was done. Chai! Kelechi must be behind this. She is the only one with a lousy 'American' accent in this office - with her 'r' inserted in every word, who knows what she taught this fellow.

My Boss has asked in his sternest voice, that I report to his office first thing tomorrow. I am dead. I can't forfeit all these perks that come with my new job role o. God help me!

My head seems to be in a quagmire of varied thoughts right now. Indeed, I need Jesus now more than ever.

27

The Zealous Sister Cynthia's Out-of-Wedlock Pregnancy!

When single ladies gather together, all they talk about are guys – if it isn't about who is getting married, it will be a 'lamentious' despair about how they are still single and 'where are all the good guys', or how useless men are or something definitely negative about the guys they are going out with.

Can't they talk about how they can get their PVCs or how our leaders are embarrassing us up and down or issues about the economy or trainings they can do to improve themselves?

Regina was determined to bring the crew down to my house to celebrate my promotion – I send am? I had planned to spend the weekend thinking of how to get Akpan off my back – he has been calling me off the hook – and get Bro Michael to... (I don't know what to say abeg, he is a complicated story).

As far as I am concerned, the crew just brought me unnecessary expenses – drinks, snacks and a big chunk of the food I suffered to cook last weekend. They spent the night and left my place all messed up.

Anyway, the visit is the least of my problems, what shocked me from the visit was the "holy Sister Cynthia's' pregnancy for a married man!

Asi: Ema!! (she shouted as she was looking for a night gown to wear amidst my things). I saw this bra in your closet three years ago!! Don't you change your bras?

Me: Abeg, the bras are still good and besides who am I changing it for, who is looking at it sef?

Asi burst out laughing

Asi: Holy Mary! Mother of God! Continue. How will you get married without a boyfriend? Don't you know you need to know whether the guy can do 'it' before you marry him?

Me: You wey dey get boyfriends, aren't we both still single and searching?

Meg: Abi o!! Even good morals don't help anymore!! Abeg, you people should come and see Mabel's pre-wedding pictures o!

"Which Mabel?" we all chorused in shock as we rushed to see the pictures on her phone.

Meg: The only Mabel we know o! The major runs girl in our school days... all the top politicians knew her.

Regina: Na only for school? She continued after school and it worked for her na – shey she landed a mouthwatering job shortly after school and now she is getting married.

Cynthia: I don't think it's fair to judge people without hearing their story sha.

She said this as she came out of the kitchen with more food on her plate.

Regina: Chei!! Everyone is just getting married. When will my turn reach o!

Meg; Abi o!! Life can be so unfair! See Mabel o! And the rest of us who thought we were better are still single and broke! Her husband looks like someone that has money.

Asi: Cynthia!! The way you are eating this night eh! Anyone will think you were eating for two.

We all laughed. Cynthia had never been a 'food person' so it was really amusing, but I noticed the change in her expression as Asi talked about her eating 'for two.'

Cynthia is one of the most upright decent Christian girls I know. She can pray, she can sing, she can do 'this', she can do 'that', what can't she do when it comes to 'church things', really?

Knowing her moral convictions very well, no one's mind went in the direction of her being pregnant at all. Being close to her, I knew how desperate she had been recently about getting married – that's basically all she ever talked about when you were with her. It was her change in countenance at Asi's statement that struck me.

I cornered her privately when the others were distracted by whatever they were watching on either Facebook or Instagram...

Me: Cynthia, you've added a little weight and your appetite seems to have increased. You practically used to live by eating air as far as I am concerned. What is up?

Cynthia: I have a baby in my womb.

She said it slowly. I was shocked! My jaw almost dropped.

Me: Will he marry you?

Cynthia: It's Mr. Maxwell.

Tears ran down her cheeks – Mr. Maxwell is a married man. I am aware that the two of them were very close. I had always considered their closeness a little bit odd. Knowing Cynthia though, my mind never drifted in the direction of the two of them sleeping together.

As she told me her pathetic story later that night when the others were fast asleep, I couldn't help thinking of my relationship with David... I don't even know how to continue with Cynthia's story right now, I am too heartbroken.

Maybe I will find the strength to continue after a good night's rest. Besides, I have two major problems on my mind - how to do damage control in the office after the new employee's embarrassment and how I am going to avoid going to my secondary school re-union. When all my class mates are introducing themselves as 'Mrs.', and talking about their husbands, children and major achievements, what will I say?

To think that I was the intelligent one with all the high moral standards... I wish Regina had not told me about the re-union - it would have been convenient to pretend not to know about it.

I really need Jesus now more than ever!

28

Damage Control 'Wife' Embarrassment

It's either you find a way to ensure we get those funders back, or you are out of here Emma!" was the first thing my boss said to me when I reported to the office this morning. I wasn't surprised; I had relived the scene a thousand times since the new male staff decided to disgrace me before the funders with his lousy presentation last week.

As a matter of fact, I had already planned to do damage control via a business lunch I had set up with the 'main man' from the funding organization anyway. I planned to actually fall on my knees before him and beg him to either give us another chance to do the presentation again or employ me in their organization (since I was sure I would be jobless by the time I failed in my damage control assignment).

I had prepared my CV and updated my profile to include that I could speak five different languages (2 of which are actually pidgin English and my local dialect, but who was asking the details anyway. I figured as long as French and English were on the list, that sufficed for a variety of languages. Who cared what the others were?).

Today, there I was sited across the lunch table with Mr. Lincoln, (the lunch I had had to dig cash out of my weekly budget to afford - really expensive lunch, I must say) and just about to answer his, "So young lady, what do you propose?" question when a very expensively dressed, heavily accessorized, aggressive looking woman (her black-themed make-up had aggression written on it) stormed into the restaurant and to my greatest surprise, walked menacingly up to us, grabbed a glass of water off our table and emptied the contents on me.

I just sat there, mouth agape, water dripping from my head to everywhere else, butt stuck to my seat, and too shocked to speak- dumb would be apt to describe how I felt, I was struck dumb.

Then, suddenly everything else happening around seemed like it was all in my dream - from some distant place, I could hear the voices of both the woman and Mr. Lincoln saying different things. I couldn't be sure if it was me they were talking to or talking about or if I was there at all. I kept thinking it was a dream, but the voices persisted.

AGGRESSIVE WOMAN'S VOICE: So, this is the useless slut you have been running around with that has made you suddenly unavailable in your house every day? You can't even pick your calls when I call you?

MR LINCOLN'S VOICE: I should pick my calls when I am in a business meeting? Why do you keep embarrassing me everywhere like this, Funmi, what is the problem?

AGGRESSIVE WOMAN'S VOICE: You haven't seen embarrassment yet. I will teach you how a responsible husband should behave since you don't know.

MR LINCOLN'S VOICE: You want me to lose my job, is that what you want? What is all this? Do you know who this lady is?

"I don't care" came her reply. "You are senseless," came his. "You are this, you are that, we are this, we are that" and on and on they continued until I realized I wasn't dreaming - this was actually happening.

It was then my senses came back and I quietly stood up, dripping hair and all, picked up my bag and was about to walk away when the aggressive woman (who by the way I had come to understand was Mr. Lincoln's wife who If I might add, was suffering from too many insecurities) said to me

AGGRESSIVE WOMAN: Wait a minute, are you not Ema, the one who carries out the campaigns against gender-based violence?

ME: Silence.

AGGRESSIVE WOMAN: (Her voice promptly changed as I saw her struggle to control her embarrassment) I am so sorry, madam, I didn't realize you were the one. I remember you from when I brought my sister's case to your office. I am really sorry Madam.

ME: Silence.

Then she burst into tears. I was so confused.

Nevertheless, my moment of victory, relief and exhilaration came in the next 3 seconds when I heard Mr. Lincoln say (whether in a bid to send me away so he could sort out his marital issues or in a bid to make up for his wife's ill treatment and abuse of me or in a bid to avoid any legal stance I may take - as if that even occurred to me, lol).

MR LINCOLN: Emma, schedule another presentation in your office, we are giving you people another chance.

That was all I needed! I hugged his wife (in appreciation for her abuse and ill treatment of me - much to their greatest surprise I am sure) and walked out of the restaurant a happy girl in dripping hair and soaked clothes. What a beautiful day.

Abeg, let me praise my God for the victory He gave me today!

Yes, I am happy that my God has come through for me again – if we had lost this opportunity with this funding organisation eh... in fact, I don't even want to think of the consequences it would have had on my career, job, position, etc. Tamuno Imiebam!

I really do love Jesus now, more than ever.

A_Ema

29

Sister Cynthia's Out-of-Wedlock Pregnancy for a Married Man!

Sis Cynthia is pregnant...for a married man. Sis Cynthia is pregnant, for a married man? Sister Cynthia is pregnant?! For a married man? I actually can't think of any way to say it to make it sound less shocking than it is. Sister Cynthia is pregnant for a married man - that's it plain and simple (or should I say plain and hard). Mmmhhh... maybe I should write it as she narrated it...

"Even the Bible says that 'hope defereth maketh the heart weak.' I am in my early 40s and I've been committed in the church for over a decade. Apart from my commitments in church, when I saw that years were running by and I was still single, I went for deliverances, prayers, sowed seeds, etc.

Most people that were (and still are) interested in my hand in marriage were either not born-again or broke-ass younger guys who were more interested in my cash than anything else – let me not even mention the married men that claim to be interested in me. As I clocked 40, my worry over my singleness increased... peoples' advice increased; 'don't select too much', 'the person mustn't be as committed as you, as far as he goes to church, fears God and loves you...'

There is the issue of your biological clock ticking away... and all kinds of guys wanting to take advantage of you – some of them feel that as far as you are 'over-mature' for marriage, you should be desperate and therefore should be willing to go out with them and spend your own money on top.

On top of that, there is the disrespect because you're still single. Even ladies that call me, 'aunty' are treated with more respect and preference because they are married. The 'bad' married ladies are considered 'automatically good' because they are married and you are looked at by everyone like something is wrong with you. Even my pastor and church members look at me with pity – I see it in their eyes.

Anyway, in this entire circumstance... I got involved with Brother Daniel. He promised me all kinds of things. He was in his third year in school then. I spent money and time on him. He was struggling financially as his father had just died - I invested my money in his education to ensure he didn't drop out from school.

There was nothing I didn't do to please him. He was forming 'being in love with me' and once he was through with his education, I became history. In fact, eh!! You know how devastated I was na - God will punish him o!

Anyway, the heart break didn't stop my biological clock from ticking continuously. One thing I found most annoying were comments like, 'You're such a fine girl, why hasn't any brother noticed you?', 'You're a very decent girl, I am shocked you are still single', 'Are the church brothers blind?' 'How come you are still single?' etc.

As I continued crying out to God in the midst of all these, Max came along. I knew he was not born-again, but he goes to church at least and is not an evil person. He was really nice to me. As a business woman, I meet a lot of customers here and there and Max stood out.

He called me often and even carried some of my shirts and men shoes to his office to help me sell. He was the perfect friend anyone could think of having. He even invested his money into my business, was genuinely interested in me and never even pressured me for sex at all.

Honestly, when he eventually asked me out, I wasn't willing to date him because after my experience with Brother Daniel who is a church brother, my dear, I didn't see how I could trust someone that is not born-again. Nevertheless, Max was persistent!!

He did everything under the sun to prove to me that he was for real and he loved me. In fact, he seemed too good to be true; he called me persistently to know how I was doing, helped me market my things even on his social media handles, was always at my place after he closes, keeps me company and helps me settle some of my problems - financially, mentally, etc.

After a few months with him being in my space constantly and friends (married and single) telling me I shouldn't let him pass me by and what a wonderful person he was, etc... I don't even know when I fell for him...

We got very close and started dating - and I was willing to marry him if he asked. Can you imagine that? Never say never o! If anyone had told me that, I, Cynthia, would date a guy that is not born-again, I would have laughed the person to scorn.

I remember the first night we had sex... it wasn't planned. It just happened. I must confess that I may have encouraged it somewhat... I gave him a lot of liberties that I should not have in the first place – we kissed sometimes, a few times I had even allowed cuddling" (she shut her eyes and water dripped down from her closed eyelids).

"I used to feel guilty sha, but I didn't want to lose him, I wanted the relationship to work so that he will marry me in the end.

One day, we just went too far and well... it happened. As he left my place after the first experience with him, I had mixed feelings – guilt and pleasure – I really loved him and enjoyed it, besides I didn't want to lose him for anything in the world, but at the same time I knew I shouldn't have sinned against God. I was filled with guilt, asked for mercy from God and resolved that it would not happen again, but...

We didn't sleep with each other often sha – but at the same time, it was not easy resisting him too. My commitment in the church definitely dropped. Even my prayer life nose-dived. I just consoled myself that if all things worked out well and we got married, I will be able to get back on track with my walk with God.

One day, as I was doing spring cleaning in his house, he stepped out briefly to buy a few things and left his phone. The only reason I picked up his call was because I saw that it was an international call. I picked up the call and it was his wife calling in from Canada!"

Imagine! His wife calling from Canada!!!! Cynthia's story just upset me. Without even hearing the last of it, I flipped inwardly - not just at the married boyfriend of hers for his wicked games, but at Cynthia herself for being so condescending.

Common! How can a Christian lady be this stupid? Every Christian female should know better. Imagine - sleeping with a guy you aren't married to, when we know how terrible these men can be and worse, knowing that the devil's plan is to ruin our testimony and tarnish the name of God.

No man is worth that kind of sacrifice in my opinion. Let me not upset myself today mbok, this story is really vexing me. As for this Max fellow, may God punish him, 'be it ever so severely!'

May be I am nasty and unfeeling, I don't know, maybe I need to be more understanding of her situation (this compromise has worked for other Christian sisters so she figured it would work for her too, besides was I not close to a married man myself?) or maybe I just need Jesus more than ever!

A_Ema

30

Do an Abortion or Face Disgrace?

This world eh?! So a babe can be busy proving to her guy that she is 'wife material' so he can marry her and the guy in question will be enjoying the whole episode knowing very well that he is married eh? Mmhhh... Wonders shall never end.

Cynthia no gree me rest o, she insisted on telling me all. She probably felt I wasn't being sympathetic enough and needed to hear it all to be fair in my judgment (as if my opinion counted in the light of the current circumstances - besides, she could never tell the story enough times to change my opinion. I had to listen anyway). Here goes....

Can you imagine - a babe who thinks she is a prospective wife, doing wifely duties in her 'hope-to-be-husband's house', picks up his ringing phone and speaks with his real wife! The only reason I picked up his call was because I saw that it was an international call – and it was his wife eh!!

To say I was devastated is an understatement. His wife and kids are in Canada and have been there for a few years. When she asked who I was, I told her, I was just a colleague o! I no fit shout.

When he got back, we had a big quarrel over it and I told him it was over between us.

He spent weeks begging for forgiveness in all kinds of wonderful ways – and my heart still yearned for him. You know Max now – the perfect gentleman, very caring and understanding – the dream guy of every woman.

I often wondered how his wife could have relocated to Canada leaving such a husband behind... Women eh! Only God knows what they need!

It was difficult staying away from him for long. One day, I just let him into my place – briefly o – and that was because he almost caused a scene outside my house since I didn't want to let him in and wasn't picking his calls.

When he got in, he begged me allow him sit down and proceeded to give me a sorry tale of how his wife and kids have been in Canada for a few years..., he didn't like the idea..., but his wife insisted.

He didn't have enough cash to visit them often and hasn't been there for more than a year. He doesn't believe that going abroad is for everyone. Their relationship was getting more distant, he was lonely, I came into his life and he couldn't help falling for me because of all my 'great and wonderful qualities' (she said this with a sneer). Long story sha. He sounded pathetic...

We continued being friends sha, but I stopped sleeping with him in spite of his constant demands.

Then, one ill-fated day - I don't know what happened - I was feeling down in the dumps with loneliness, thinking of my sorry plight and wondering when this journey to marriage will end, my mother had called lamenting how her enemies were laughing at her because her first daughter had not married (she had just been returning from a friend's grand-child's naming ceremony), my customers had delayed their payments, I was broke, etc. He came to see me, met me in tears and gave me his shoulders to cry on... the rest is history...

The relationship is definitely over now sha – after the devil has succeeded in ruining my life, I guess. I am in my forties, so I cannot even think of an abortion. I have reconciled with God, but I haven't been able to go to church at all.

God forgives, but humans do not. I am thinking of relocating or going to the village until I give birth... I am so confused. I thank God for my mother – she is just happy about the prospect of having a grandchild from her first daughter – she is my support now.

I haven't told Mr. Maxwell yet...

Life can be confusing – I am somewhat secretly happy about the baby (at least if I don't get married, I now have my own child), but at the same time I am thinking of the consequences of my action to myself, the church and God. It will take a while to build my spiritual life up again.

Suppose Rapture had taken place when I was involved with him or he had died in my place one day or I had even died in my sin? I shudder to think of what God delivered me from..."

I listened to her story and was at a loss for what to say. My resolve to be done with David is stronger – I don't want wahala in my life abeg and the devil is really evil.

I'm just thinking to myself: if Cynthia aborts this baby shey no one will know and she will still be seen as a 'good 'Christian sister. We condemn the repentant 'pregnant' sister and look the other way at unmarried brethren who are sleeping with each other. The sin is not in the pregnancy but in the fornication. Life sucks sometimes!

Desperation to get married is from the devil – and I am definitely going to put a stop to Mr. Akpan's disturbance. If I follow desperation and marry him, I will regret it for the rest of my life. As for Brother Michael, I don't know what to make of him – sometimes he seems really interested in me and at other times, he is just aloof - in spite of all the green lights I have been giving him.

All these 'holy' church brothers sef, maybe because they have got used to being without a female, so the urge to get married isn't there anymore.

I'm kind of confused here about even the reason I am still single; is it that not everyone is destined to get married or maybe there is something I am not doing right or maybe I am not praying enough - I do not know.

What thing I am certain of is that the Bible says, 'What shall it profit a man, if he gains the whole world and loses his soul.' Eternity is real and I definitely want to make it to heaven – single or married.

As a result, I will do my best not to allow myself get so desperate to get married to the point that I compromise my Christian principles, so help me Holy Spirit.

I need Jesus now more than ever!

A_Ema

31

Every Day Issues of a Single Lady

Man and woman wahala no dey end. If I follow man-and-woman wahala, I won't think of anything else. Other issues are on ground.

The politicians are acting drama for us – and for people who are condemning the government and do not have their PVCs yet and or not planning to vote... they shouldn't complain when the party they do not want wins the elections.

The other day, I was involved in a conversation/gossip about Regina's Bro who broke up with her on the grounds of, "...it was not God's will..." He is married to someone else and is going around telling people that he didn't propose to Regina, they were only just close, he made no promises, etc. Can you imagine that?!! (May the good Lord judge him according to his works). Wonders shall never end!

Why can't all brothers be like Bro Felix who finished his Youth Service and two years after, got a job and married the sister in the church whom he had been friends with even before he graduated?

In the meantime, Bro Michael whom I am 'tripping' for is not even 'saying' anything. Once in a 'red' moon he calls me to know how I am doing and sometimes after evening service, when he is not carried away by all the sisters in the church (who are all seeking his attention I am sure), he walks me to my bus stop.

I am not ready to spend the rest of my years waiting for a fantasy or a crush that just won't grow, I'm looking elsewhere biko.

To my relief, Akpan has stopped calling and texting – I guess he has got the message at last. I could go on and on if I didn't have other issues on my mind.

Office wahala is my biggest problem now. Imagine my grossly incompetent staff (woman I have to put up with) that is always late, never meets her deadlines and does shoddy jobs, having the effrontery to humph and whine about unfair treatment.

Sometimes, without going through the office procedure she doesn't even show up at work! When I send her queries or confront her, she turns my words around, verbally attacks me and goes about telling people how inconsiderate I am – she has children to take to school, her child was ill and had to be taken to the hospital, she doesn't have a house help and I am aware of it...

Her excuses can go on and on and then she ends with how it's because I am still single that's why I am so wicked and inconsiderate and what makes me think I will get married when I beef married women out of sheer spite and envy? I tire. Yesterday I heard her clearly say in reference to me.

INCOMPETENT STAFF: I am not surprised she isn't married. With such a bitchy nature, how can any man tolerate her? Jealousy will kill her one day. My brother can never marry a female like her.

So said the lazy incompetent, unqualified-to-work-anywhere woman who by the way personally begged me to help her get this job just a year ago.

PS: The brother in question (who I am to cry over because he can never marry a female like me) is a cleaner in the Federal Secretariat. I'm sure if I get to 80 and I am still unmarried, I wouldn't cry over that loss.

If she was the only married woman I've had to work with maybe I would think she was right about me, but she is not and I've seen others who behave more professionally and are efficient.

Really, to be a boss while being single and working with people who just won't do their jobs well is an upheaval task.

The next thing you know, they are calling you names that are synonymous with 'hard' and 'bossy.'

Is it such a difficult thing to send me a text that you won't be available at work because your child is sick? In fact eh! She just shows up whenever she likes without letting me know why; when I react, she complains to the whole world that I am 'insultive' to my elders. Respect is reciprocal o!

My own boss is pushing me to get my team to deliver on researches and data collection for our job. If I cannot get my unit to deliver, my adulterous supervisor and her driver boyfriend will be only too happy to have me disgraced before the branch manager as an incompetent leader (why am I attacking her adulterous activity sef, after all, her husband who is far away in the U.S is probably cheating on her too. I guess the goose and gander fit each other just fine).

On the flip side, I have begun my search for a new house – a bigger one-bedroom apartment – and it's such an odious task! In fact, I don't think it's a woman's job. Maybe I should just stop the cold shoulder act towards David and ask for his help with this... bad idea. I will be encouraging him back into my life and I am not ready to end up like Sister Cynthia mbok.

I will give that assignment to Bro Michael – shey he acts as though he were interested in me? In the meantime, I will sow a seed in church towards our church building project so that God will lead me to the right house and neighborhood. I've heard enough stories of 'demonic' landlords, lands and neighbors. I also need a place that has relatively stable water supply and LIGHT! I believe that God will do it for me.

On a positive note, a friend of mine who I respect a lot and who is above 40 years old is getting married soon!!! There is hope for people like me o!!

Before I forget! I got an email alert from an old flame from over 10years ago when I was doing my youth service – Andy. Could it really be him? I heard that he got married to a white lady for 'Green Card'

As I hope his marriage story is a lie, my heart is already fluttering with excitement... It has been over 10 whole years and I'm still emotionally excited over him... mmhhh... When I get to the office tomorrow, I will check my mail on my desktop to confirm; my phone is kinda acting up now.

I really need Jesus now more than ever!

A_Ema

32

Andy - The Return of a Ten-Years-Ago Love Affair

6:30am

I am so sure that even if I was married and Andy showed up from the UK, I would have sneaked out of my husband's house just to meet him (ok, I would definitely not commit adultery sha, lol).

First love is really something o!! To think that we didn't even sleep with each other and I still feel this excited in spite of the over-10-year separation. Just the knowledge that I will read the mail from him today has got me feeling so good inside – for some crazy reason, my yahoo mails are not synchronizing and dropping into my phone, so I must wait till I get to work - agh!!!

I am even wearing one of my best office clothes and I've given my make-up special attention this morning. I no fit laugh!! Will he see my dressing as I am reading the mail? – I am laughing in Greek!

8:45am

The first sight to greet me when I stepped out of the house on my way to work was my freshly-battered-faced smiling young neighbor. Obviously, her husband had beaten her up again - probably while the rest of the sane world was still asleep.

There she was smiling at me like there was something she had over me - I just couldn't figure out what that thing was (I'm pretty sure she can't be assuming being married to a guy who beats her for a living, places her in any position over me). That guy is going to beat her into the grave one of these days, and I'm sure she'll go in smiling.

I refuse to allow her dampen my feeling and also refuse to allow my Mrs. Late-Coming bug me either - it's 8:45am, she is not in the office and I haven't got any text from her. I understand that she is married and has kids, etc, but she lacks the little official curtsey of letting her Team Lead know when she will be coming in late (or not at all) – that is what annoys me.

10pm

When I got to the office today, I felt so happy that I refused to allow Mrs. Late-Coming (by 10am! Can you imagine?!) without-permission annoy me; Kelechi was to do a research on the whole issue of Female Genital Mutilation and she submitted a scanty document, I held my peace… I gave the job to the intern to do.

I know that for the next one week I will be working late to improve on the assignments I gave to some members of my unit. It's about time, I called for a formal meeting of everyone in my unit to set and agree on ground rules and penalties for defaulters. I will not come and kill myself because of work. I also didn't allow all these dampen my joy…

Most of the time, I usually have a hurried lunch so I could get back to my desk (work pressure), but today, work pressure or not, boring meetings or not, once it was 12noon on the dot, I shut everything and everyone out, went online to read my mail…

With all my excitement, it was just 2 lines.

"Darling, how have you been? Really missed you. Send me your mobile. Will be in Nigeria in a couple of months."

Just 4 short sentences! I really don't know what I was expecting. Why can't guys just write/say more? Must they be so brief?

Anyway, no time for fuse – the major thing that is making me over-excited now is that he is coming into the country very soon and I have sent him my mobile number. In fact, from now on, my phone will be so close to me – I don't want to miss his call for anything.

Trust me nah – I sent him an epistle in reply, lol. I didn't say much about myself though – if not he may see no need to call me again.

I wonder if he is still born-again – towards the end of our Youth Service year his Christian life was already shaky.

O Lord, please help me! I just want to settle down and get married to someone I love and who loves me too. Surely that is not difficult for you to do. Shey Jesus said, with you all things are possible? Please, have mercy on me and let Your Word just come to pass in my life.

When I think of all my male friends, Andy is the best of them all and I will choose him any day... but this UK he has gone to... is he still born-again? He didn't even indicate if he was even married yet and he isn't on Facebook (I won't even mention Instagram). As I await his call, I still feel all happy and so excited that I heard from him at all – even if it was just a 2-lined mail, lol.

I really need Jesus now more than ever! A_Ema

33

Church Issues 1 – Where do the mature-singles belong in the church's 'natural' groups?

Na wa! No wonder single ladies get desperate enough to marry 'anything' as long as it comes in 'male trousers' (even if they have to take care of him, provide for the home themselves and still get beat up every day) because even in the church they are being side-lined/don't belong anywhere.

The family prayer meeting in church today just made me more aware of the fact that people like me belong nowhere (we are not located anywhere on the family tree).

Prayer points for families were being given and all the prayer coordinator kept saying was; 'Let us pray for our families. Let us pray that God will bless and protect our wives, husbands and children..."

Does family mean only wife, husband and children? For some people in the congregation, family means parents, brothers and sisters o! How do these members flow with the prayers when you are only asking them to pray for their spouses and children?

How is it that mature singles have no formal 'natural group affiliation' in the churches they belong to (Mary and Martha were mature singles na and they had a place in the life of Jesus).

After service, various natural groups were asked to wait behind - youths, married women and married men... I am not married, and definitely much, much, much older than the people that make up the youths group (a lot of them there even call me 'Aunty'), so I figured quite naturally that I should be on my way home.

I really wonder where the mature single person come in within the 'natural' or 'family' groupings in the church.

As I was leaving the church after the family prayer meeting today, one of the ushers accosted me and asked why I was not waiting behind for the youths meeting. Hian!! At my age?!

A number of reasons came to mind, reasons I wondered he couldn't figure out for himself

1. I am older than they all - the least of them will be 30 and I will soon be 40!

2. I taught most of them in the Children's Department and they call me 'aunty' even as they are now in their twenties.

3. They will definitely be uncomfortable having 'Aunty me' in their midst.

4. I am tired of being in the youth group - which I had joined donkey years ago.

I wanted to read out these reasons to him and ask him if he was blind but I went with the more noble excuse of, "I am in a hurry" - all the while wondering why it was me he saw to ask; weren't there other mature single sisters/brothers (especially sisters) who didn't bother with the youth meetings too anyway.

In spite of the fact that the mature single brethren don't really have a 'place' in the church, we do most of the church work. I am not complaining o. If one is single and does not use his/her time in the service of God efficiently, is it when they marry?

Nevertheless, something must be done about this somehow. In spite of our dedication, some key roles are not assigned to single ladies because of the single status.

For instance, when the children teachers' coordinator relocated and left the church, in spite of the fact that I am one of the teachers that have been in the church the longest and more readily available and have a good relationship with the children and their parents, the position was left vacant (probably because the other married ones were not so dedicated to the work) until Mummy Ib came into the church.

She was with us for only a few months and promptly became the head because 'she is married' and has 'children.' Apparently, I am not a good example to the children (especially the teenagers), me being single and all. After all, "if I were a decent girl, shey I should have been married by now, abi?"

When admonishing youths about the need to serve the Lord, resource persons usually end their exhortation with, "... today God has blessed me financially and I am married with 3 wonderful children."

Is it that those that served God in their early youth age (or from their teens) and are now in their late thirties and forties and still single have not been blessed by God? Or those that married as virgins or good Christians and for years are without a child are not blessed too, abi? It's all pretty confusing.

In the meantime, this Andy fellow hasn't called yet and Brother Michael is helping me look for a house. My phone is ringing; everybody should just leave me alone abeg, I have enough problems of my own.

Jesus is indeed all that I need!

A_Ema

34

Church Issues 2 – 'Thinking' my Miserable Single Life!

I am here 'thinking my (single) life' and my phone wants to disrupt me. It is not as if whoever is calling will bring me a husband. Let it ring mbok, I dey think my life. I don't like picking calls when I am 'thinking my life' it cuts into my thought process and hinders the flow. The person calling isn't even serious anyway - just called twice...

A woman's life is really something o! She no marry or she marry late, wahala; when she marry, she never born, double wahala; she born sef and she born only girls, make she just prepare herself for another dimension of problem... God will help us.

As I sat in church as the prayer session was going on (you no say we no dey tire for prayer for Naija, our problems too much - plus village people) I kept waiting for the prayer sessions that were related to me and the children I teach in church - I waited till my ears turned red.

It was all prayer points and prophecies related to financial and marital problems (fertility, infertility, better jobs, financial breakthrough, marital through, contracts, etc. I just tire). My children and I waited for them to remember that they needed to pray for success in their exams, admission to tertiary institutions, peer pressure issues, the effect of disoriented families on the children, etc.- no one remembered o.

As I left the church this evening after the family prayer meeting (after escaping from the usher), one of the lead male choristers gave me his number and told me to give him a call when I get home.

Hian! All these church brothers... what does he want me to call him for? I am sure he wants to ask me for money. I am trying to rent and furnish my own house o - I don't have money to dash anybody now. I just got paid and it is almost gone - all these money-monitoring-spirits...

I am too exhausted to call him today; office work was exhausting - arranging reports to give to our funders, trying to ensure that the office runs smoothly when I am away on a training trip to Abuja, settling unnecessary disputes among colleagues, etc.; I will call him tomorrow abeg! Let me drag myself to get something to eat.

****

I am finished! The calls I missed was an international call - UK number - and definitely Andy. Chei!!! What kind of rubbish is this eh?! Why will he choose to call when I was 'thinking my life?'

The devil is a liar! I bind and cast! The love of my life called and I was... in fact eh! To think that I have been keeping my phone close to me all these days and he didn't call; it was when I was not in the mood to pick calls and was getting tired of waiting for his call that he decided to call.

Now, I don't have enough credit to call back, I have not subscribed to mobile banking and shops are closed! It will be embarrassing to flash him. What do I do? Send a text? No, I will check if his number is on WhatsApp and then send him a message.

What is up with me anyway and what makes me think it is even Andy sef? Really, I tire eh!! I will just check if the number is on WhatsApp, send a message and go to bed.

It has been a hectic day. I hope I will not sleep off as I have my quiet time this night. To think that they say being single gives one free time to pray and do everything else - they should rephrase it to, "when one is single and unemployed (or probably running one's own business)."

A lot of the time, it is tiring combining work, church commitments/activities and one's personal life together. One gets home totally exhausted at the end of the day. If protection at night or good dreams was hundred percent dependent on a quality night prayer session eh, people like me will be in big trouble indeed.

I still need Jesus more than ever!

A_Ema

35

"Na Dem Dey Rush Us O – Mature Singles Like Us"

Over-mature-for-marriage-single-ladies like us, na dem dey rush us o! My soon-to-be-married senior friend (in her 40s) paid me a visit over the weekend to involve me in her wedding plans. The way the guys are rushing her now eh, it's not today o - even she sef tire!

She is a very serious Born-Again Christian who doesn't joke with her walk with God at all. She is even a pastor of a branch in her church and preaches holiness like hell is just beside the door (maybe that's why she is getting married late - the brothers probably thought she was a dispassionate person devoid of emotional feelings - but then, what do I know?).

Anyway, she gave me gist of how the brothers have been rushing her since her engagement was announced. One came and was like he had always liked her and had wanted to propose but could not because he didn't have a good enough job and he was waiting for the right time to propose - now that he has a better job, he heard she is engaged.

Another one (a missionary) told her categorically that God revealed to him that she is his wife and so has to marry him - how she is good for the ministry, will be a good partner for him, etc.

Where were all these guys since? Now that she has been swept off her feet by a very loving Christian man, the suitors have begun to emerge from strange places (are these ones not the enemies of progress we keep hearing about, trying to distract her from the good thing that has come her way?).

Why do these things happen anyway? Is it just the devil trying to distract someone from her marriage plans or is the first person from the devil and the later ones, God's agents set to direct one away from the devil's plans?

The question now is, should she abandon her fiancé and marry the missionary? The guy is so persistent!!

The guy who wants to marry her is about 5 years younger than she is and practically worships the ground she walks on and to spice it up, he is financially stable. The missionary is broke - that's all I can say!

It's her salary they will be surviving on until somewhere down the lane when he will probably be transferred from the village to the city and after a few more years, members will now bring 'seeds' unto the Man of God as appreciation gifts or in expectation for what they desire.

Abeg, she is in her forties and these 'years' for when her missionary-husband will be able to comfortably take care of her are too long for her to wait for! As for the other guy who is lamenting as if he is about to lose some mega millions because she is about to get married, no one is even thinking about him.

He had known her long enough to have made his move if he really wanted to - and he never said anything... he claims he was waiting for the right time, he was trying to work up the courage to speak to her, he was this, he was that... infact, let him pack well joor!

Ladies in their forties (and even fifties) these days don't look as old as our mothers did in their time; I wonder what has changed? Make-up? Classier ways of dressing? Civilisation? Who knows!

Also, single ladies even in their forties look like they're in their thirties - maybe it's the fact they haven't given birth yet or that they do not have marriage hassles stressing them - so you see young guys seriously hustling them for marriage (abi are they just looking for older females to replace their mothers? Who knows? One can never be too sure these days, so much shenanigans going on everywhere). It is well!

In the meantime, Andy has called!! He said he missed me and I have always been on his mind. He will be coming to the country very soon and will give me the date!

The only issue I have is how he could love me so much as he claimed and yet still get married to someone else (for Green Card, I guess). They are divorced now...

In fact, the heartbreaking news is that his faith seems shaky. Most of his Christian convictions have flown away with the wind - or whether it is the cold from the snow that froze them. Chai!!

What do I do? Brother Michael seems to be interested in me but is not saying anything in that regard. Is it that when these guys get born-again all their chaiking skills vanish? Tomorrow, if I marry the guy who isn't born-again - but has wooed me long enough and proved his love for me in many ways - they will say I have derailed.

We all still need Jesus now more than ever!

A_Ema

36

I Don Tire for 'Near Miss' Marriage Proposals!

I danced today. I don't mean danced on a stage or to an audience or in church or wherever else dancing takes place, I mean I shuffled my feet in excitement because I will be away from work for a while on a trip to Abuja again, and this time to stay at the Transcorp Hilton Hotel!! (Why shouldn't I dance?).

Most of my colleagues who also got the invite won't be attending for several reasons; because of transportation cost, (chei! I miss GEJ! When he was president of the country, there was hardly any fuel hike that led to high transport cost), children's school fees and expenditures for the new term, husband says he too will be away from home so who will stay with the kids through the period, because this, because that...

So once again, being single, free and self-dependent gives me the upper hand; I better enjoy this my freedom for as long as I have it o!

The icing on the cake and even more exciting than Transcorp is the fact that I will stop by to visit and lounge for a whole night in my friend's luxury apartment in Abuja (her husband bought it in her name! Can you imagine that?! Some wives are enjoying! I must go there o! Let me too follow and taste what leaving in wealth feels like).

We were classmates back in secondary school and as boarders who stayed in the same hostel, it's like we are sisters. Although we don't really talk often, we know we've got each other's' backs.

So there I was shuffling my feet in what I called a dance as a result of my trip, when that intern in my office who I am older than with donkey years (and who has been trying to ask me out in annoying ways; I have just been pretending not to notice) had the mind to ask me if he could accompany me on the trip so we could 'have time away from work to bond'!

These small boys eh! If I were married, would he have had the nerve to be asking me out? If I had my way, it's to put him on my laps and whip him for disrespect! Nonsense! I am sure his transport bill will be at my expense. If he thinks that it is every mature single lady that is so desperate to get married and will be willing to be with anyone to achieve the 'Mrs' status, he should think again.

Most of these small boys who are after mature single ladies are only interested in the cash they have - whether they end up getting married to them or not. God should just do and answer my prayers and bring my husband soon o! I don tire for insult from people who were still in diapers when I was in secondary school. In short, I don tire completely.

All these near-miss marriage proposals sef; is what I am going through not what these deliverance ministers call, 'near-success syndrome'?

First it was Akpan (too local, uncouth and his grammar...agh!), then Godwin (who wants sex before marriage... abeg o, I am heaven bound! Suppose as I am sleeping with him in the 'hope' of 'let-him-marry-me as "I have waited 'loooong' enough for marriage", the trumpet sounds and I miss the Rapture?

I shudder at the thought; or what if I even get pregnant sef - what will I tell my teenagers that I preach to or the church or the unbelievers around who look up to me as an exemplary Christian lady, I shudder even more! God forbid!

I know how the devil works. Others may be doing it and getting away with it, but the day I land 'in bed' before marriage, he will spring up and ensure I am disgraced. Abeg, I no fit shout.

There is Andy - (his own story is complicated - backslidden, divorced and my emotions are running riot over him - why won't it anyway, he is my best male friend ever!).

In fact eh, I have tired! At this point, I should change my marriage prayer points. I will think of what to change it to - or maybe I should even go for one of these Mountain of Fire and Miracles deliverance programs; I don't know much about all these warfare prayer points and I need them now!! For crying out loud, the years are running!

This one that Kelechi is deputizing for me and will be running the office in my absence... I need prayers. I hope she doesn't spoil my work or my name with her evil intentions.

Enough of thinking about problems abeg - Transcorp Hilton, here I come. As other civil society actors will be attending the event, who knows, I may just meet 'someone.'

I need Jesus now more than ever!

A_Ema

37

I Almost Died Today

I woke up today very excited, not because I was grateful to God for one more day, not because all those I loved were still alive and well, not because I was healthy and sane (not that all these things weren't good reasons to be grateful for), but because I was visiting my friend who lived in so much luxury.

I couldn't wait to let some of that luxury rub off on me; I was visiting my friend in her luxurious 9th floor apartment which was almost the 'toppest' floor of the building she lives in.

Her husband had bought her the apartment on the 9th floor for a birthday gift and I was excited at the prospect of enjoying a little luxury. Also, I was arriving Abuja today and I would be lodging at Transcorp Hotel - the training starts tomorrow and I intend to spend this night at my friend's place.

I finished my morning ritual of taking a bath and brushing my teeth; I didn't bother with breakfast because who would want to fill up their stomach on any food (no matter how good it tastes) when they could keep it empty enough for luxury food (as far as I am concerned, any food eaten in a luxurious apartment tastes better than any other) and I stepped out.

My flight was uneventful and I just kept smiling throughout the journey and didn't stop until I got to her luxurious estate and stepped into the elevator to ride up to the 9th floor.

Two seconds after the elevator took off, PHCN did the usual - power went out. If anyone had told me when I woke up excitedly this morning that I would die today, I would have burst into tongues to return that statement to sender. I had actually heard of the 'getting stuck in an elevator experience', now I was going through it.

No one pre-informed me that phone networks went dead in an elevator (they probably never thought I would get stuck in one), no one told me oxygen would run short in a short pace of time, no one told me Nigeria was not prepared for such emergencies, no one told me I would die today (OMG! I would have eaten my breakfast or the snack I was given on the plane and at least died with a full stomach).

I banged on the door and screamed for help as loud as I could as my mind began to run through all the scenes the story of my life comprised of;

I thought of the Transcorp Hotel I am supposed to move into tomorrow morning, I remembered Kelechi would be excited to take over my position in the office, I remembered I was going to be meeting with Andy soon (we have been communicating regularly), I remembered Bro Michael's and my relationship (which was probably all in my head by the way) and saw my dream of spending my life with him fading away.

I remembered I had not won enough souls to get stars on my crown in heaven, I couldn't remember if I had any issues with anyone that could bar my entrance into heaven.

I remembered that bowl of ice cream I didn't have yesterday because I didn't want to gain weight (I should have taken two bowls had I known), I remembered that I wasn't totally free from the financial obligations of the new term (some of my church children were depending on me for their school fees and other school expenses).

I remembered burials where they write 'Glorious Home Call' on the poster; who would describe my dying in an elevator as glorious? I remembered 'soooo' many things...

As my mind continued going through all these myriads of thoughts, my breath was ceasing and I gasped for breath as the oxygen was depleting (at least it felt like it was) ... I felt death pulling me towards it.

At the feel of death, I banged harder on the door, screamed louder, sweated more, cried more... suddenly, power came on and the door opened on the 6th floor. I flew out, right into my very surprised and frightened friend. She was surprised to see me or anyone else coming out of the elevator looking like a dead rat.

My friend: Ah ah, babe, what happened to you?

Me: Panting

My friend: Why are you soaked; did it rain on your way here?

Me: panting

My friend: What where you doing in the elevator, I got tired of calling you and waiting for you and decided to go down in case you didn't remember it was the 9th floor.

Me: You were going down to look for me, why didn't you use the elevator?

My friend: Na wa for you o, nobody uses that thing here o. Where is the light for that one in Nigeria? We always use the stair case. That thing is a death trap.

I almost slapped her. No one had told me to avoid elevators in Nigeria that were not in hotels or shopping malls, no one had told me I couldn't exploit every form of luxury within my reach, no one had told me the rich used staircases (I actually assumed they walked on air and rode elevators all day long), no one had told me I could have died today and no one would have helped.

I just got up and took the staircase right back down to the last floor and walked away to my hotel room (I am never visiting that my friend again!). My friend is still calling me; I haven't picked her call - I could have died in her luxurious building today, you know.

I love Jesus now more than ever.

A_Ema

38

What if rapture takes place when I'm diverting company funds or lying in my report?

Wonders shall never end. See me envying my friend in her luxury only to realize that there is more than meets the eye. I keep telling myself that I should not be moved by people's 'Facebook relationships', but I still keep failing all the time!

She called my phone to almost battery-dying-point until I finally picked!

How did the conversation even start sef? Ok. I asked her about her husband and she was like, "That one na husband?" Immediately she said that, I called room service and ordered food up to my room. I knew what was coming already - gist about how terrible her husband is.

Have you noticed women never say anything but what is horrible about their husbands and marriages? I tire. I'm not saying they are gender slaying o, I just kinda wonder if men are really scum or the women just wanna believe that.

Anyway, after a sumptuous meal (for I have always advised myself to make the most of whatever meal is placed in front of me before any woman talks me deaf with her marital problems. It's just not fair to subject my ears to that much pain on an empty stomach. My ears can't 'think' properly without food in the stomach; yes, my body is connected that way), we relaxed and talked.

...... what is paining me now sef isn't even my friend's story about her husband o (when I'm in a more retrospective mood, I will delve into that); it is that I could not enjoy the training I came to Abuja for very well because of office issues. Kelechi will not kill me! I kept dashing out to attend to calls...

First of all, a representative of one of the international donors that is sponsoring our rural women campaign and support for domestic and sexual abuse came to the office by 10am to get the report on the first phase of the program and Kelechi was nowhere to be found! She had not come to the office - by 10am and with no explanation given to the project officer!

If that was all, the problem could be solved easily, but she wasn't even picking her calls and I got to know from a colleague that works closely with her that she had not even written the report at all!!

Already, these international organizations don't even trust us as Nigerians; it would seem to them that we had eaten their money without doing anything at all. We needed the balance of their money to complete the program in the rural area we are implementing the project in.

We had promised the rural women that we would empower them financially, now this catastrophe!! These women really need help. After waiting for about thirty minutes - when all our delay tactics to get Kelechi on the phone had failed - they left (and I hope not in anger o).

By the time Kelechi got to the office around 11am, she told me that she had urgent family matters to attend to and I won't understand.

I had wanted to do the report myself o! However, she categorically told me that she will handle it and had added, 'Why you dey like to do like sey na you know too much? Emma, abegi, you too dey do like say na you dey work pass.' This is the result of my delegating things to her!

My only joy was that I heard she came in with a swollen jaw (hopefully, she got beaten by one of the women in her by-force-husband's life - imagine what I am wishing? But really, she has a penchant for attacking the 'other' women in his life).

My gratitude to God was that the intern, who keeps acting like he and I were made for each other, joined us to the village and I had told him to take note of everything. I quickly called him to write the report as soon as possible.

I persuaded my boss, with all the apologies I could gather from everywhere, to call the donors back and tell them that Kelechi had really urgent family issues to attend to – taking advantage of the fact that everyone respects the importance of family.

They agreed to come back in a few days - but didn't say when. I hope they can still trust us. My hope is that I have worked with them several times and have never failed them before, so they would make exceptions.

The only reason this incompetent Kelechi is even assisting me at all is because the founder of the NGO is a close relative of hers - or else, she would have been sacked long ago. Did family issues stop her from writing the report and keeping it ready before the day she was told the representatives would come for it?

I spent the next few days calling the office to follow up on everything. Although the organization has agreed to come, I wonder when they will come.

I cannot blame them for their distrust sef. Even at this meeting/training we are doing, of all the 20 NGOs that came only mine and 2 others completed our projects faithfully (from the assignment from our last meeting some time ago in Benin) and I was the only one that even gave them back a refund of money not spent! I got accolades for that, lol.

It is important to me that I have a clean record of honesty and integrity. As a Christian, it is very important. Jesus said we are the light of the world, so even in my circular work, I try as much as possible to do what is right. Cutting corners and diverting funds illegally are not my thing at all!!

Jesus is coming soon - suppose the trumpet sounds when I am diverting funds illegally or writing a lie as a report? Abeg, I no fit shout! I don't want to miss the rapture and besides, even if the rapture doesn't take place in my lifetime, I want to do my best to be found faithful to God on 'that' day of final reckoning.

Funny enough, my suspicion regarding Kelechi's 'urgent' family issue was right. A colleague called and told me that she had been on a mission of trying to catch her husband red-handed as he was on her (at the risk of her job?).

She was up and about town trailing the activities of her philandering,   not-really-her-husband-co-habiting-partner she insists is her husband - even though God and everyone else knows her hand, leg or any other body part for that matter have never been asked for or given out in marriage to anyone. I don't know what to say abeg.

I was given the full gist sha, but that is not what is paining me now. I have prayed that our donors will just see the whole incident as a one-off thing and come back so we can fulfill our promise to the rural women and young girls.

The plight of these rural people that I have gone to get myself involved in is the one that is worrying me now. The report is ready; my fingers are crossed.

Jesus I need you now like always.

A_Ema

39

Transcorp Hilton Hotel Thief

Note to self: Luxury is a beautiful thing. Don't let anyone tell you otherwise.

Ah!!!!! My Address two weeks ago - Transcorp Hilton Hotel, FCT, Abuja, Nigeria, Room...!!!!!! I wish that were my permanent address. Ah!!! To lounge, to bask and to soak in luxury. All that talk about 'no place like home' is what those who live in grand castles tell the rest of us ordinary folks so we won't aspire for comfort.

Believe me; there are a million places better than home (case in point- Transcorp Hilton Hotel, FCT, Abuja, Nigeria, room...). Abi do I have Sauna that comes with the package in my home? Or a well-equipped gym? Or such a beautiful pool (which I spent time staring at in wonder but never getting in - as I am definitely not getting in any pool with everyone around watching me: no one is gonna get a glimpse of me for free).

Or such comfortably soft beds that lure you to sleep with no 'I pass my neighbour generator' blasting by the window specifically to ensure you don't sleep? No, I don't have any of that, so I reiterate 'there are so many places better than home (if Heaven is better than that place, then I had better go to Heaven. In fact, I must go there. All those who keep arguing 'there's no Heaven' are on their own - me wanna go there).

Anyway, I guess I had to pay for all this comfort and bliss somehow, because someone stole my purse (with 'everything I am', in it - Atm, ID, Cash...) right in the hotel of bliss.

I never knew people walked into hotels like these, slipped into conference halls and pretended to be part of the training or seminars or whatever went on, just so they could participate in the tea breaks, lunches, get Per Diems and whatever Transport Refunds they can lay their hands on.

Nigeria!!!!! It is bad enough that anyone would engage in such a despicable device, but to take my purse along with the tea break, lunch, Per Diem and T.R is taking it way too far. Even the CCTV cameras couldn't catch the pro that did it.

The whole thing is so painful (if I hadn't got a dinner coupon for an extra day after I checked out of the hotel as a compensation, I would still be crying by now).

What's gone is gone anyway, and what's done is done. I am back to my 'home' and there was no light when I arrived - of cause.

My only joy is that immediately I walked into my compound pulling my box behind me, I bumped right into my neighbour (the one who usually looks at me like she was better than I just because she is married - even when she was all battered and bruised by her husband), who tried to give me that I-am-better-than-you look again (this time, one tooth was completely gone - and her right eye was shut) - this time, I was prepared for her.

I pulled my box right under her nose so she would see the Transcorp Hilton hotel sticker (which I had taken off the reception counter for this purpose and tagged to my bag immediately the taxi dropped me outside my gate) I had on my box and the one I had deliberately 'accidently' stuck to my dress with a pin.

Her condescending look and fake smile froze immediately she saw my stickers and for once I was the one who gave her the, 'I-am-better-than-you' look (after all, I am pretty sure the only places she ever got to travel to were the market and her husband's village).

As I drove into Port Harcourt from the airport, I began to re-appreciate Governor Wike again. Anyone that says that he should not come back as governor for the second tenure should go and hug the Ex-Governor's monorail and see how it feels. If all the governors in the country (and the ones that take over from them) continuously do strategic things to improve their states, this country would have been a better place for us all.

In the meantime, our elected politicians are busy acting Nollywood movie for us 'up and down.' Let them continue. Shebi another election is coming and they will come and deceive those that they will deceive again? Mschew!!!

I have been able to attend to most of the issues that arose in my absence. I personally called the representative of the organisaton and from our rapport, it was obvious that all was forgiven and they will be coming to see us. I am so relieved!!!

Ah, Life is good!!!!! It has never been better. What a triumphant week for me - forget my missing purse and all.

If Jesus is all that we have, then He is all that we really need. Jesus now more than ever.

A_Ema

40

Social Media Relationships 1

Dear Diary, I know I had said I would never visit my friend again because I almost died in the elevator. However, since I couldn't resist the urge to spend a night in her luxurious apartment, I went back but this time, I took the stairs. I enjoyed the luxury for a night, I cannot lie. I would have had sweet dreams if not for the stories of her marital problems.

Me: Whatever you think of your husband, he has tried for you! This house and everything in it are so beautiful!

My friend: My dear, this house? It was after I got my brothers to threaten him regarding the evil way he treats me and made them tell him to get a house for me in my name that he did it – he just tried by offering it to me on my birthday.

Me: I don't understand... ok... just start from the beginning.

My Friend: When we got married, in the first few months, it was heavenly. Since he obviously had so much money, he told me to quit my job and he would pay whatever it was my company paid me per month - I agreed.

Few months after I gave birth to our first child, he changed. He stopped giving me money for upkeep and he even started following me to the supermarket to buy my cosmetics and other personal things for myself and the baby – the only things he currently gives me money for are food, household items and money for my hair.

If I talk for long on the phone, he will ask me if it is the feeding money I am using to buy credit to talk for so long. He uses the money he gives me to insult me. I dare not mention even sending money to my parents. The jeep I drive and the expensive clothes and jewelry he gives me are for his public image.

Public image is important to him o! When we go out together to functions, I have to play the part of a happy and contented wife and he acts so caring and loving and says all kinds of wonderful things about me.

By the time my second son was born, I decided to quit crying and going into depression and just concentrate on my children.

Me: I hope he never physically assaulted you.

My Friend: He tried it na! I forgave him twice, but the third time he tried it, I gave it back to him and informed my brothers. After my brothers' intervention, our relationship got worse, but at least he never beat me again. I just leave like a slave in the house. I have no voice – except the one I raise on my children.

Me: Have you tried getting a new job?

My Friend: Ah! How nau? I tried secretly, he got wind of it and blocked it – shebi he has money and connections? What I do now is put money aside - from the feeding money - for myself. I want to raise capital to start a business which I intend give my younger sister to run for me. If I can earn my own money at least, I won't have to rely on him for money all the time.

Did I tell you that he not only sleeps around, but also even brings his girlfriends to our home! Once in a while, I have had their voices from the direction of the guest room. Mmmhhh... I have suffered.

That one is even small, the most embarrassing time for me was when I saw him and his steady bitch of a side-chick on the same plane I was boarding to PH when I travelled to pick up my certificate from Uniport - he has a major bitch he sees more regularly now.

My friend and I saw him hand in hand with his babe, like two love birds. We ran into each other and there was no show of remorse from him at all! He turned away and they both walked past me! For someone that likes 'public image', I was shocked.

My friend was soooo mad, in fact, she had wanted me to give her the go-ahead to cause a scene at the airport to teach the bitch a lesson - I didn't think it was worth it at all.

When we got to PH, he even carried her luggage to a waiting vehicle (something he doesn't do for me – even when I was pregnant) and they both took off together, while I was busy arguing over taxi fare with taxi men.

To think that I had even used a few months to save up money for my trip because he refused to give me and to add salt to injury, when he returned from his trip, without me referring to the incident, he lashed out at me for travelling... details for another day my sister.

Me: Wasn't he a Born-Again Christian when you married him?

I asked this because I know very well that my friend was a serious Christian and couldn't even imagine that she could marry someone who wasn't Born Again.

My Friend: That is another matter entirely. Anyway, is it about being a born-again Christian? A sister in my church, who is a chorister, married a guy that is not born again and her marriage is bliss. I see all her Facebook and Instagram updates and pictures and besides, he follows her to church every Sunday and even picks her up after her choir practice and midweek services.

People that have visited them attest to the fact their marriage is good. He is the regular gentleman who likes giving a helpful hand whenever he is called upon.

Sometimes, I think of the other brother in church that was interested in me and who I turned down because this one had financial security – I was tired of suffering. Besides, when people saw my husband and all he had, especially my family members, they were convinced I had made a good choice.

Me (thinking): Facebook updates ke? I'm shocked my friend could conclude on the blissful state of someone else's marriage based on Facebook updates when her own Facebook updates always shows so much bliss, yet here she was, painting a gruesome picture of her reality.

I was listening to her story, raising my eyebrows in shock, gasping in amazement while my mind was scanning her Facebook page and all the wonderful updates that spelled a forever honeymoon kinda marriage in Dubai and every other foreign land she had posted her 'awesome hubby' had taken her to.

The most outstanding update was the recent one she wrote for their wedding anniversary - "It has been seven awesome years with you. Though we have had our ups and downs, I will choose you over and over again."

Then she pulled me out of my wandering with the shocking question "How far for you and settling down na? Hasn't anyone come yet?"

Seriously?! It was shocking because in the light of what she was going through, one would expect that she should be warning me against marriage or cautioning me to be extra careful in my choice (abi does this woman secretly hates me and can't wait for me to join the vicious circle of suffering-and-smiling-on-social-media wives?).

There is a lot to say, but NEPA has taken light and I don't have enough fuel in my generator...

Truly, Jesus is all we need now and ever.

A_Ema

41

Social Media Relationships 2

Me: But I still ask, was your husband born-again at the time of your marriage?

My Friend: He was not o! My dear, like I said, it is not about being born-again. A bad man is a bad man. He was a good man when we met and the type that goes to church on Sundays sha.

Me: So why did you marry him, considering the kind of Christian you were?

My Friend: Na advice o! I was already in my thirties and no reasonable person was coming forth and he showed up. He was really very nice and romantic – better than the church brother that showed up later, shortly after I had met my current husband.

Since no one was coming, he seemed like the answer to my prayers and I was tired of waiting, my biological clock was ticking and everyone around me was convinced that he was the answer to my marital prayers.

Me: When you both were dating, were there any signs that he would be like this?

My Friend: None o! The only thing I can say is... come to think of it now, he was particularly gentle-manly and very romantic when we were in public...

Me (thinking): So, in spite of what she knows the Bible has to say about this, she still took the risk of marrying someone who is not born-again? That a friend of ours tried it and it is working for her does not mean we should all venture into risky ventures (not that it matters though.

I know the husband of this friend of ours well and at a child dedication after-church-party, I saw him throwing in some alcohol into his son's soft drink; he said it was to get his son to be strong).

When I mention 'born-again', I am not referring to people who 'say' they are, but people who truly are and will not commit sin even in private (these days, everybody is 'born-again'), for all the other categories of 'born-again' it is time that exposes them.

Me: With all the maltreatment, unfaithfulness and verbal abuse to dent your image of yourself, why are you still with him then?

My Friend: Na wa for you o! Divorce? God forbid! Is he beating me? He thinks that I am still with him because of his money – he has thrown those lines at me now and then – but he is so wrong. I have to think of my children and besides, I am here for the long haul! Marriage is for life my dear.

When she asked me about when I will be getting married, I was mute; trying to figure how to answer her question and trying to merge her nightmare with the marital bliss updates she posts on Facebook...

My Friend: I know some Men-of-God in Port Harcourt I could recommend to you for prayers. The problem with you is that you do not take these things seriously. Even when we were inviting you to these prayer places back then, you refused to come. I don't know why you do like you don't have problems.

Me (thinking): If it is those places you were visiting that finally gave you this husband, thank God I didn't follow you mbok. Me, I don't have the liver to suffer this kind of ill treatment and still hang around in the marriage. That is how they will be going to church, be workers in the church and still be visiting 'seeing-road' prophets and prayer houses - na wa.

My Friend: Ema, God works through different ways. We have to find ways of getting solutions to our problems. After all, it is still God's name they are calling. They may ask for certain things that may not be in line with what you are used to – but is it not solution you are finding? You will not leave your church o! My dear, menopause is knocking at your door o!

Me (thinking): If she is so good at finding solutions, why hasn't she tried to find a solution to this current menace of a marriage from the 'solution providing places' she visited to nab the man in the first place?

My Friend: If you don't want that option, I know a few guys I could recommend for hook up, but the problem with you is that you over-do things. You are almost 40 and getting to menopause. Let it not be that after waiting on God for marriage, when the marriage comes, to born pikin will become a problem. I know a few mature single ladies who have an issue or two out of wedlock – deliberately so, just to avoid stories that touch.

Me (thinking): I am so hungry, when is this autobiography gonna end?

Me (aloud): Are you saying that the whole point of marriage is for children alone?

My Friend: Ah! What else na! If not for my children, will I still be in this marriage?

We talked through the night and as we were preparing to sleep, she threw in the last question:

My Friend: Will you be attending our class re-union?

Me: No!!!! Please, I want to sleep o!

My Friend: Haba! This is our first and it will be fun to reconnect, let our hair down and just have fun again.

How do I explain to her that I hate school re-unions! Word from the grapevine is that these so-called re-unions is an exhibition for classmates to show off their marriages, kids, husbands, accomplishments and money; leaving those of us who haven't achieved whatever it was they felt they had, to lament our fates. While others are introducing themselves as 'Mrs. ...', I will now be the only one still 'Miss...'. Chai!

If it was a mixed school sef, I would have, maybe, just maybe, considered going – perhaps some of our male classmates (who are born-again) may still be single...

I knew that a new conversation with her will resume in the morning. I shut my eyes and acted as if I was asleep.

In spite of all that was going through my mind, I am still wondering, what makes men change negatively towards their wives after marriage; one of the women they sleep with that used evil charms over them, something bad their wives did (even for this, can't they forgive?) or maybe they get involved in cultism.

Like this my friend, I'm sure her husband is in a cult that told him not to treat his wife well once she gives birth. What can I say? What do I even know?

Indeed, Jesus is all we need!

A_Ema

Dates and Events That Depress Me – Including School Re-Unions

There I was, lying in bed this morning, smiling because everything that seemed to have been going wrong at work when I was away (curtsey Kelechi of course) was on the right track again. I had met with our funders who had agreed to fund our rural outreach and put a smile on the faces of these rural women we work with this Christmas – It felt good to be making major contributions to humanity.

I had had to push everyone at work extra hard to get on the right track after our major blunder (Kelechi's blunder I mean).

I had set new ground rules for my team members - zero tolerance for lateness, incompetence, sleeping at work and a lot of other things that every other organization practiced (but you can be sure they all hated me for it, talked behind my back, claimed it was because I had no one to love me that

I was so hard and intolerant and a lot of other things I really don't give a flying saucer about).

The result was that we got back on the right track with our funders and that's all I really care about.

So, there I was, eulogizing myself when my phone rang and my friend (the one with the terrible husband called me, with information that reminded me about the days I hate (sometimes I think that girl's friendship is guaranteed to keep me depressed).

Me: Hello, madam, watagwan?

My friend: I hope you remember our secondary school reunion is coming up and I don't want to hear you are not attending. You need to learn to have fun, you aren't getting any younger. Besides, the year is almost over and I am sure this will be your first fun event this year …bla bla bla bla bla…

And just in a few sentences, she reminded me of the days I hate most; My Birthday, Christmas, and Reunions.

These 'bad' days remind me of my condition in life. As Christmas approaches and the year draws to an end, I am reminded by everyone around me that another year has ended; I am not married and my financial status is still struggling to rise.

When my birthday comes, the voices of those who keep reminding me that my biological clock is ticking, that I am getting older and I am not married yet – not even engaged – and my chance of giving birth to children is reducing, keep playing in my head.

Now, they want to depress me with a school re-union. It's twenty years since I left secondary school. What do I have to show for it? Nothing!

Dressed in their expensive clothes, my class mates will take flights or drive in with their jeeps, talking about their CEO and top positions in their various businesses or jobs and how they are trying to balance their executive jobs while managing their husbands and children; and what will I say? I go dey look like person wey escort others come world.

In addition, I am sure that some may just come to the re-union to show off sef! I blame them? If I had anything to show off at all, won't I be looking forward to attending? I see their Facebook and Instagram updates and pictures about their happy and comfortable lives (ok, I know I am learning not to trust all these Facebook and Instagram updates and pictures – but they can't all be deception, can they?) and I know for sure that they are all doing well.

This world I come so, why is my story the negative one? Why can't I be the one running my own flourishing business or having some top executive position in an oil company and going for summer holidays outside the country with my husband and kids?

Anyway, I told my friend categorically that I will not go for the re-union; my excuse was I didn't have enough money for the venture - which was true sha. I promised I would send in my little quota for the project we want to do in school only.

Ah! That one, she refused to hear o!

My Friend: Nonsense! These days, networking is key! You don't know who will be of help to you and school alumnus are good support bases. Besides sef, it will be fun! We can forget all our problems, let our hair down and feel like teenagers again!

It's good for the health. You that needs sponsors for your NGO work, don't you think our network will be of help to you? Whatever my husband says, I will go o! He cannot beat me. Abeg o, I cannot come and go and kill myself.

Me: Didn't you hear I said I don't have the cash?

My Friend: Do you think I have it myself? You know my condition now, but I will find a way, even if it means selling something in the house! Oya, before you do like I don't want to help you, I will find a way for 2 of us.

I didn't answer her, but I know I won't go! We chatted a little and she finally hung up.

Come to think of it, is my life situation that bad? Am I worse off than others? Let me count my blessings and see what I've got.

BLESSINGS' CHECK LIST

1. Life

2. I have a good job and just got promoted (it would have been the worst thing ever, if I were single and then jobless)

3. I now have an official car attached to me

4. A family that loves me

5. I am Heaven bound and committed to God's work

6. My official trips have made me sleep in great hotels across the country – La Meridean , Protea Nicon, Transcop, Reiz, Corinthia Villa... (Na Oriental I dey target now)

7. I have met and had face to face discussions with top politicians and foreign ambassadors

8. I am healthy (and don't even have to take anti-depressant peels)

9. I have developed myself academically and professionally

Who says these aren't worth thanking God for? Perhaps, my story isn't so bad after all.

I need Jesus now more than ever. He is my friend, my king and my ever-present help in time of trouble.

A_Ema

43

Andy Proposes – I Weep for the 'Marriage Error Decisions' of our Twenties

This brother Michael, if they sent him, he should tell them that he didn't see me!

I told him to help me look for a house to rent and send pictures via WhatsApp, he has flooded my gallery with pictures of not only one-bedroom flats, but 2-bedroom flats in expensive places like GRA and locations in PH that I had no idea existed (seems he even dared to send me pictures of houses in Lekki too.

I can't understand what I could possibly be paying rent for a house in Lekki for, considering I live and work in Ph. This fellow is beyond me. Wonder what I ever saw in him.

I cannot afford those kinds of places. Even if I could, 'they' said it is not good for a single lady to look too 'financially accomplished' so that she doesn't look too self-sufficient and scare away well-meaning guys that may want to marry her.

It is bad enough that I have an official car and a driver – I don't want living in some expensive place to come and spoil my market. Already, my driver is rude and insolent – he probably hates taking orders from women (and worst of all a single one at that) – it's about time I relieved him of his duties sef.

When I get to church later in the week, I will confront Brother Michael personally – or does he think I have some millions stashed somewhere?

Come to think of it, is that why he has been showing interest in me (I know I used to have a crush on him sha, but I am over that especially as he refused to see all my green lights)? Not even one-bedroom, two-bedroom apartments! Hian!

Anyway, that's by the way. I am... I do not know the word to use now. Should I say confused, unhappy, sad? It's all man wahala o!

Andy and I have been having a wonderful time over the phone. He calls me via WhatsApp regularly and we speak for at least an hour, lol. Things have been going on very well until he dropped the bombshell.

Andy: It's amazing how about fifteen years have gone by and we still feel strongly for each other and we can still gist and laugh like time and life haven't passed us by.

Me: My dear!

I sighed to myself. This is the guy I should have married. I am more comfortable with him than I have been with any other guy in my life. Fifteen years have gone by and our connection is still there. If only there were mobile phones and Facebook back then, we would not have lost touch... he would not have married someone else, become divorced... as he talked, I felt a pain in my chest...

Andy: The main reason I want to come into Nigeria is because of you. I know I messed up big time. I should have married you, but I was not thinking straight. I was not sure you would accept me, so I never asked and besides, my mother figured that a lady from my tribe would be a better option.

My darling, we can correct the mistake now. I believe God has shown me mercy by giving me a second chance to be with you. I loved you then (though I never said anything) and my feelings have not changed...

Finally, though, he just told me to think about it and when I'm ready, tell him what I think.

When we hung up, I buried my face in my pillow and cried holding my aching heart. I cried for the mistakes we make when we are young, the wrong turns we make, our youthful foolish choices, my present state – he represents and is everything I desire and want now (love, romance, marriage, financial security, etc.), but just don't think I can get because it is in the wrong package.

Andy is not the only one living in regrets. A lot of people are married today to people they had no business getting married to because they could not speak out to the 'one' they truly loved or they were using wrong criteria to choose a spouse and left the one they truly loved (or who truly loved them) out in the cold, etc.

Now, years later, when they are more mature and especially when they are having a hell of a marriage or divorced, they remember the one they loved or who loved them, but they let them go.

… I am not just guessing, I know this for a fact because I have married friends (male and female) who have expressed their regrets to me – for reasons I don't understand, they seem to trust me enough to confide in me.

I too have my regrets – I probably would have told Andy how I felt about him; but our culture does not allow it and it would have been a terrible risk because in spite of what he is

saying now, I know for sure he would not have married me –
he liked 'slay queens' and I was the 'plain Jane.'

I don't want to think about what I feel for him – it's not good
for my spiritual health. I only know that I am hurting inside
and wishing all kinds of things.

My neighbor's generator is really annoying me. Why can't
they buy a better one? The noise is just unbearable! I'll make
sure I don't forget to see Brother Michael about those
apartments – or get someone else to look for a house for me
(or better still do it myself) because this brother seems to
think I have a lot of money.

Come to think of it sef, isn't the whole idea of a single lady
living 'big' out of date? I know a family friend who built her
own house, owned a car and was a top officer in some big
bank and in spite of it all, she got married.

They have been married for about ten years and I've not
heard any negative story about the husband (except the
usual stuff – adultery and little arguments here and there).
She had told me that she almost didn't build her own house
because people were advising her to wait until she gets
married so she won't block her way...

Although, honestly, some guys actually date and even
wickedly marry seemingly 'financially stable' mature single

women basically for their money – as their own form of 'hustling' to make ends meet. May God punish those kinds of guys be it ever so severely…

My heart still hurts; if Andy is not born-again, what do I do, what do I say to him, how can I turn him down? Deep down somewhere in the corners of my heart, I wish the words Andy was saying to me were all coming from Brother Michael…

…but then, I know that if I had to choose (forgetting the born-again factor), I know I would choose Andy above everyone else. Life really does suck sometimes!

Jesus is really all that I need!

A_Ema

44

A Beautiful Day – Guess Who Finally Beat Up Her Husband?

I wish that all my dreary, boring and upsetting days' end as beautifully as today ended. Amen.

PS: This is actually a prayer, not a wish- hence the 'Amen' at the end of the plea.

Today started as one of those upsetting days for me. It rained this morning, I got stuck in the flood that usually follows even the slightest drizzle in PH city; my driver kept his face like driving me was the worst job on earth (he has no idea he is about to lose his job, once I get the new driver I have applied for - I just dey laugh am, his days are numbered).

No one had arrived the office by the time I got to work, the papers on my table were wet from the obviously leaking roof and ceiling over my table (I won't be surprised if it was that Kelechi girl who bore a hole in the roof, just to get my table wet. I hope I am not getting paranoid here).

To make matters worse, the intern who thinks he is God's gift to women and has a right to being the future Mr. Ema (as there is no chance I will be taking his name if his wish to marry me ever comes true in his dreams), strolled into the office at 9am and had the effrontery to poke his head into my office and say "Hi babe" (I think I will send that fellow a query this week or sue him for harassment). I was upset all day.

I got home early from work so I could cook only to realize I was out of gas and I couldn't prepare dinner. Hunger was slamming me left, right and center. I couldn't even drink garri because I had no sugar. Then to make it worse, I began to hear sounds from my neighbor's house that told me her husband was at it again - beating her blue black.

I don't get why this neighbor of mine keeps staying with this Mike Tyson of a husband and always has the gall to look at me like she has something better than I have. Anyway, since I flashed my Transcorp Hilton profile at her that day, she hasn't dared to look down on me again.

I was so upset by their sounds that I picked up my heavy frying pan and headed for their house - I just wanted to knock the breath out of that bully of a man today; if the wife hadn't had enough of his beating, I had had enough of the sound of it.

To my greatest surprise, their front door opened immediately I stepped out of mine and someone was thrown out. The person fell backwards unto the wet ground and behold the person that fell was my neighbor's husband, the almighty Mike Tyson.

His head was bleeding and he was whimpering in pain, (and I swear could see fear and shock in his eyes). His wife stepped out after him, a heavy frying pan in her hand. She kicked him again and again.

I stopped in my track, mouth open, eyes popping. She stopped and looked at me and my frying pan, gave me a slight nod, I nodded back and she gave her husband one last kick.

Just like that, my day was made. I wasn't hungry anymore. I feel justified to say I had one of the best days ever.

Apparently, women who get hit or beaten by their husbands can actually hit back, the men just don't know it. They think they are so strong yet they never consider entering any tournaments except the ones that involve beating women.

Apparently, women just let the men hit them because they think it's a man's prerogative. Apparently my neighbor had decided it was her prerogative to give him a little dose of his own medicine today. Apparently, I won't sound like a good Christian if I say, "I am very proud of her."

PS: 2 hours after he got beaten, I peeped out and found the now sober husband, washing his car himself - the same car he used to make her wash for him every morning before he went to work (what a scallywag!!!).

Jesus now, more than ever.

A_Ema

45

Different Pastors, Different Prophecies

(for the same problem o)

3pm

The chief usher in the church just called me to tell me that one of the senior pastors in the church wants to see me. When a pastor wants to see a single lady, there is only one thing he wants to see her for – to ask her about her 'marital condition' or give her some revelation or prophecy about her marital situation. I'm not looking forward to this meeting, besides, I am tired of them.

All these pastors wey dey see road anyhow… when someone has an obvious in-everyone's-face challenge like being a matured single person, childless or your child has a major psychological or health challenge, they will tell you all kinds of things about the demonic reason behind it, to even prophecies with exact timing on when your breakthrough will take place (and the time passes, you're still waiting and the prophecies with dates of manifestation still keep coming).

For the single ladies, it is either there is a covering over her, or a spiritual husband is holding her down or some wicked person from her father's or mother's side is working/standing against her marriage.

When they are done telling you all kinds of demonic reasons behind your problem, they will come and give you donkey days to fast for and do night vigils.

See me o! I don't have energy for long fasting and vigils – I don't want to stress myself to the point that I look too miserable to even attract any guy's attention or I won't have the energy to do my secular job. I have only one source of income – I neither have a husband, boyfriend or father who will be giving me extra income.

I am so not looking forward to this meeting. Let me get back to work. We are preparing for our visit to give support to the rural women we had visited a few months ago.

10pm

Brother Michael and I couldn't see in church today – he was rushing off for some appointment, besides, I had to see the pastor.

The meeting with the pastor was amusing. I was right; he had a message from the Lord for me concerning my marital situation. I really don't mind what he said eventually, but what is amusing me is the conflicting messages...

My Pastor: ...so, please be patient. The Lord wants you to know that He is preparing someone for you and in the fullness of time, he will come forth. Do not be in a hurry to accept any proposal – it seems that there is someone knocking now, be careful.

Me (thinking): Relief! I had thought it would be something demonic with instructions for a prolonged fast or vigils, lol.

However, just last week, a guest minister that came to our church categorically told me that there is a wicked woman in my father's house sitting on top of my marriage and with my permission, he would decree and she would not live to see the end of the month.

He had brought me out and asked, "Should I prophesy more?" That was a bad move of his – I told him, 'no' categorically clear. I saw the shock on his face. Usually, the response is usually, "Man of God, prophesy!"

Anyway, I am thinking of the two messages... being amused. At this point, which one should I hold on to?

I have also received prophecies that came with dates of 'prophetic manifestation' as to when I will get married; the dates came and passed and nothing happened – I am still as single as single can be.

I honestly do not understand these things, but one thing I know is that every child of God should have a personal walk with God, should know how God speaks to them and thus will be able to discern. When we get to this point in our Christian lives, prophecies will come basically confirming ministrations we have got from God ourselves.

Also, with all the prayers we pray in church, the devil is not so powerful abeg. Christians have to learn how to pray and when to stop attacking demons and stand on God's word (or the personal promise God has given them) in faith that what He has said concerning whatever situation they are going through will come to pass.

All this running after different men-of-God (especially the ungodly ones) for solutions and prophecies is not doing any good. The Lord did not restrict His power to only pastors.

I believe what my pastor said sha – as he spoke about the 'knocking' on the door, I knew it was Andy.

A relationship with Jesus is really all that we need!

A_Ema

46

Fulfilling Destiny

The time out with the rural women was awesome. It was nice to put smiles on these women's faces – at least with the skills they have acquired, they could get other sources of income; it will help them a lot this Christmas.

One thing (amongst others) that makes women stay in physically abusive relationships is their financial dependence on their husbands. If they are empowered financially, they will be able, to a large extent, to take a better decision on the matter – which will not be only based on financial support from their spouses.

Anyway, the smiles and joys on their faces made all the inconveniences around the outreach worthwhile. There is nothing as good as finding your path in life, affecting lives positively and helping to shape people's destinies for the better. It gives one a sense of fulfillment.

I really hope it will not be written of me when I leave this earth that "she got married, had children...' and that would be all. In the Bible there are stories of people that just "begat" God knows how many children and that was all that was said of them – may that not be my portion!

I'm also thinking of my children (that is the ones in church and around me whom I have spent almost 10years nurturing). Some of them are graduates now, others are in higher institutions, secondary schools and even paid employments.

In the course of my daily running around, I stumble into some of them (especially those that have left secondary school) and I can see the depth of joy and gratitude in their hearts when with broad smiles they greet or wave excitedly at me and or give me a bear hug and sometimes verbally express their gratitude for all the advice, scolding and beatings I gave them. The joy I feel at these moments can't be quantified!

What almost spoilt my time out was one obnoxious fellow who I am sure will go around 'scandalizing' my name by telling everyone that I'm the one that doesn't want to marry just because I didn't roll over the floor in gratitude to him for wanting to marry me after we just met for one day! Tomorrow, people like him will be the ones saying that people like us like to 'select' too much and that's why we are still single.

He was the team lead of the N.G.O that partnered with us to implement the project with the rural women. We talked the first day to plan the activities and that was all o.

The next day over our dinner, he started asking me personal questions about my age, qualification, salary, ex-boyfriends, etc. He told me how much he loved me and believes I am the one for him, etc. When I told him I needed time to think it through as I didn't know him at all and we needed time to get to know each other- his response:

Him: What do you want to know about me? I have told you everything about me already. Listen, I want to settle down early next year and I know you are my wife. You have spent your nights crying and praying to God to send you a husband; now he has sent you one, you are turning him down. What do you ladies want? A guy that will come and lie to you and deceive you? Baby, I am for real.

If that was all, I won't complain much, but what annoyed me most about him was the way he kept shouting and giving me orders (like he owns me). If he had any doubts regarding my responses, he would categorically tell me how I was lying to him.

He still calls me now and If I miss his calls, he would scold (very rudely too) and ask me who was preventing me from picking his call by 10pm (he never let the thought that I was probably asleep cross his mind).

We have not even started going out and he is constantly accusing me of not being true to him. The guy has trust issues (probably the reason he is still single at 45).

When we talked about 'husband beating' issues, his opinion was that women should be careful about how they talk to their husbands. Hian! I am already late in marriage, let me not come and marry and be miserable on top.

Some guys just think that because a lady is 'over-mature for marriage' (in their opinion, that is), she should settle down with anything that is called a man. As far as they are concerned, we should just agree to marry any man that wants to marry us or else we will be labelled as being 'choosy' or not ready to get married. According to him, he is God's answer to my prayers – so is marriage the only thing I pray for? He should park well o!

I am even querying his born-again status because though he says he is a committed Christian in his church, he wanted us to divert some of the funds for the women to our individual pockets as team leads (in addition to the extra income we are already getting for the work we are doing)!

Tomorrow, we will accuse the government for being corrupt. Who are those in government anyway? In my opinion, they are the already typically corrupt everyday Nigerians that divert funds in their offices and carry out other corrupt vices who have eventually (and probably 'corruptly') got their asses into the seat of power!

I just dey look am – I am trying hard to act nice because I don't want 'bad name. The next time he calls or mentions coming to visit me (I don't bring guys 'I am not sure of' to visit me – tomorrow if I am raped, the society and the police will blame me and look at me as the encourager of the rapist), I will tell him off finally.

PS: If you know him, tell him to stay the flying saucers out of my sight.

Anyway, before I spoil my good mood... a life of fulfillment is really worth it – no money beats the smiles of gratitude on the faces of people one has impacted positively and the lives God has used one to help mold for the better.

Jesus is truly all we all need!!

A_Ema

47

Another Christmas is Here Again… I'm 'Planless' and Still Single. Can Suicide be an Option?

So, another year is coming to an end eh? It is well o. What happened to all our hopes and dreams for the year?

As I see parents buying things for their children, I wonder how married women who do not have children feel and I wonder how I feel myself as I have no plans at all (thank God I have no village to be afraid to go to lest the village people try to make me feel bad about the fact that I am not married).

It is well... another year is coming to an end and a lot of people are getting discouraged about all their unfulfilled desires and are worried about the hope of the coming year.

This is one of the things that draws crowds to end of year church programs. Imagine that I missed House on the Rock's 'Experience' because I was at the Redeemed Camp! Before I used to attend both Shiloh and Congress; these General Oversees are not trying at all – this year all three programs held the same day!

To think that in spite of this, there was still a crowd in all three programs - na wa o! There is really a maddening crowd in this nation – no wonder jobs cannot go round (PS: if this many people are in church and claim to be Christians, who are the people destroying this nation?).

The frustrations and depressions are real o - people are committing suicide 'upandan,' including a lady in one of our branches who attempted it because she is still single and as broke as broke can be. They say she is in her 40s (but looks like one in her 50s to me) and she is working as a teacher in an ought-to-be-closed-down school and not earning up to 20k.

What made her finally decide to take her life was when her boss, who is younger than her (and who specializes in insulting her for any mistake she makes), gave her the insult of her life and an indefinite suspension with a possibility of sacking her. I heard it was the boss' words that really got to her.

I don't' blame her sha, but in my opinion, being a very broke spinster is not the worst thing on earth. Life throws shit at people now and then; so, should we all commit suicide? Perhaps the following people should commit suicide too

1. The jobless lady whose working husband beats her, doesn't give her cash and flaunts his girlfriends in her face

2. The lady who has been married for over 15years, without a child and her husband and in-laws are giving her major heat and treating her like shit

3. The family that has no place to lay their head and rely on goodwill from people to eat

4. The father who has been amputated and is bed-ridden with no money to pay his medical bills (the feeding and school fees of the children is not even considered)

5. The lady who lost her husband and kids in one singular accident

6. The lady who is the bread winner of the family (with a minimum wage salary) and the husband is lazy and abusive

7. The family whose rented house got burnt down (due to their own fault) with all their belongings; the list can go on and on

Life has ups and downs; we should just rise up to whatever it throws at us, face our own individual challenges squarely, enjoy whatever each day brings and hope for better things.

If we all look at the challenges and private midnight tears of many people, we will realize that most of us are going through major stuff – single, married, rich, poor, disabled, elderly, etc. There is no need committing suicide over yours no matter what it is. I've even heard of a wealthy man who actually committed suicide over money issues at the bank.

This sister from my church was saved from her suicide attempt; she was rushed to the hospital and the drugs were taken out of her system – something miss am!

No matter how bad a person's situation is, there is something to be thankful for one way or the other.

The year is coming to an end and I am still single in spite of all the prayers and prophecies - however, at least, I have had a few interests; even though they are all 'wrong' choices. Also, at least, I got a promotion, salary increase, slept in nice hotels, have been able to reach out to more people through the Nonprofit work and I got more souls into God's Kingdom this year.

Very importantly, my family is all safe and sound (in spite of the near miss in a certain airline recently. Airlines in Nigeria are the worst!). Indeed, I am thankful to God. As for the marriage issue, God will do what He will do – sometimes, I get tired of praying about it sef.

I am also thinking of Andy's offer. He has decided coming to Nigeria isn't a good idea for him. Whether I decide to marry him or not, he still loves and would like to see me, so he has decided he would send a return ticket to me to visit him in the UK. All he needs is a go ahead from me and we will decide when.

I'm still trying to articulate my thoughts on that – the major issue here is the sleeping arrangement.

Me thinks to myself, to go or not to go? Perhaps, I should take his offer. What will I lose? I have female friends in the UK and I could sleep over at their place – to avoid stories that touch (Ps: I know I cannot get married to Andy because he is not born-again, besides, the way we feel for each other eh, there is no way we won't have sex). In fact, this Andy sef, abi dem send am after me?

Jesus still, more than ever.

A_Ema

48

Was That Really a Marriage Proposal?

10pm

Mmmhh... it's amazing how someone prays for something and when the answer comes, one is confused as to what to say or what to feel. You have always felt you would jump in excitement and joy, but when the day comes, you become numb – in words and feelings. How do I start?

I met Brother Michael finally over the house matter.

Me: Bro. Michael, this one that you are sending me 2-bedroom apartments... that is not what I asked for o! Even the one-bedroom apartments you sent, seem expensive to me. Abi, did you go to Lekki to snap those pictures? (I asked laughing).

Brother Michael: Has Pastor spoken with you?

Me: (confused) What has that got to do with the apartments? I speak with Pastor a lot, so you have to be specific.

I am the 'functional' Children's department head as the 'positional' (married and with children) one is not always available. I guess the church feels uncomfortable allowing a single lady run the department that a lot of married (with children) women are also involved in.

Anyway, what is my own in the matter? Mine is to do the work I believe God has called me to do – church politics is not in my calling.

Brother Michael: Did he discuss any marriage issue with you?

Me: (thinking: he does that sometimes, so I don't even concentrate when he is talking about it anymore). Please, what is your point? How much do the apartments go for?

Brother Michael: (he paused for a long while and said slowly and quietly) Please, see Pastor again. I intend to pay for any of the 2-bedroom apartments you like because we would both be staying there together if you agree to spend the rest of your life with me. You could manage where you are staying until after the wedding or if where you are staying is really that bad, the one-bedroom...

Me: (thinking); I was stunned. Is this supposed to be a proposal? I remembered – the pastor was talking to me recently about praying concerning my marriage partner as someone was coming; I thought it was just one of those normal words of encouragement.

Brother Michael: So, what do you think?

I said something that sounded like, "that's a flattering proposal" "Let me think and pray," "I'll see Pastor as you have said…" I hardly knew what I was saying.

I am sitting here with the sound of generators (my neighbour's and mine) blasting through my thoughts. I don't know if I gave him an appropriate answer since I don't even know what I said. I am not even sure of what I heard him say.

Was he serious or just pulling my legs? I am not even feeling excited – I just feel numb. I will go to sleep and when I wake up in the morning, I'll call him back – by then my head will be clearer. I am going to sleep now – let me call the new security guy to help me put off my generator.

9am

Now, I am excited and bubbling with great joy! So last night was for real? Brother Michael actually proposed!

I woke up this morning feeling still uncertain, but with a little smile playing around my lips at the thought that one of the most eligible bachelors in the church (whom my feelings have had all up and down moments with) actually made an attempt at a marriage proposal to me.

At about 8am, Brother Michael called.

Brother Michael: My darling, how was your night?

(Darling ke? These men sef, them too do. They start with acting like they are romantic just 2 seconds after proposing, then a week into the marriage, they throw the drama out the window and show their true stony hearted character. Anyway, me sef will pretend like I am fooled by the act. When time reach, all of us go show our true self)

Brother Michael: I hope I didn't startle you yesterday. I am really serious about wanting to be with you for life. I hope I will get a positive response from you soon. Enjoy your day.

I appreciated his gesture for calling and we hung up. I feel so excited right now! I wish I could take the day off. This is a wonderful Christmas gift!

I doubt that the several programs I had attended in December and the fasting and seed sowing are behind this blessing, God has planned times and seasons and apparently, this is the time for me. I give Him glory.

Pray ke? I had already prayed to God about Brother Michael and I know what the Lord told me – it's just that I had given up on him since I was not sure about him anymore especially with his aloof attitude and all.

Now, what do I do about my London trip?

Jesus is really all we need o!

A_Ema

49

That I'm a Christian does not mean I'm not a human being with blood flowing through me

I saw the Ghanaian actor Mawuli Gavor today (I mean on screen, I didn't see him up close and personal) and I paused for a while and I asked myself, "why can't I get a man as hot and handsome as this to propose to me, why can't I be the victim of a proposal from such a man."

What was my crime that the Mawuli Gavors of this world couldn't see me? Brother Michael pales out in comparison to Mawuli Gavor, in fact there is no comparison. Apparently, I thought I was thinking these thoughts, I didn't realise I was thinking out loud until I heard "Sister Ema!!!!" It was sister Maureen who shouted my name in surprise.

I had stopped by at Maureen's house and we were watching a movie on Africa Magic Showcase and Mawuli Gavor was on the screen.

I really wasn't particularly watching the movie sha, but immediately he hit the screen, I was glued to the screen and to make it worse, the soundtrack in the film was a very old song from the 90s – 'Mysterious girl...I want to be with the woman that I love.'

I just began to imagine I was the woman that Mawuli Gavor loved and I didn't realise I was speaking out loud until sister Maureen called my name. Then I said again

Me: Mehn!! Check out this hot guy! If this guy attempts asking me out eh, the Lord will have to arise on my behalf to stop me from following him straight home.

Sister Maureen: Sister Ema!! How can you be saying this? I am shocked! If anyone had told me you could say a thing like this, I would not have believed it!

Apparently, I succeeded in shocking Maureen out of her wits because she looked really shocked.

Sister Maureen: Holy sisters like you don't look or sound like you have emotions na! (she said this laughing though).

I had no idea people looked at me like some emotionless bat; I don suffer. Apparently, everyone assumes I have no eyes to see beautiful and handsome people as if I am some sort of drone.

That a lady stands on the altar and preaches about the eternal reality of hell and the need to be holy does not mean that she is not a human being.

I hope the fact that I am with Mike has changed or at least will change that opinion of me. The Mike sef tire me, very boring unromantic fellow. He finds it difficult to send texts - at worse to send one expressing his feelings for me (the day he does this, I'll kill a cow).

Even when I go out of my way to look good, I wonder if he even notices (well, once in a while, he will just smile when I ask him how I look). When he is like this now, how will it be when we get married? (He is so lucky I didn't meet Mawuli Gavor up close and personal).

Everyone to whom I have complained about Mike says I shouldn't bother myself. They insist that unromantic men are the best and romantic men are Casanovas whose Christianity can't be trusted.

The logic seems quite odd to me, but what do I know? After all, I have never been married before. They could be right though because there's a whole lot to successful relationships beside romance.

According to Mrs. Jumbo (an elderly married woman in my office who I respect a lot), there are basic questions one should ask oneself when it comes to relationships. In her own words, "My dear, the questions you should ask are:

• Is he there for you when you need him to be?

• Does he support and encourage you?

• Does he share the same Christian beliefs and convictions with you?

• Does he fear God?

• Can you rely on him to help you in time of your need?

• Is he resentful towards your family members?

• Does he respect you and what you stand for?

• Is he ready to motivate you to succeed?

• Is he a kind-hearted person?

• Does he have an authority over his life that he respects?

These are the basic things you should be asking. What if he doesn't send you texts or calls you ten times a day? What is the point of having romance when he will not respect you and be supportive towards you?"

I think she is right because I've noticed that some of these sweet-talking guys are even very unreliable.

I guess a lot of the time, we get carried away by superficial things and lose the right man for us. Nevertheless, that does not mean the guy should not try sometimes nau! It can be frustrating – he will see your 'missed' calls and will not call till hours after (sometimes you will even be the one that will call hours after). What will be his excuse? "I was busy and I intended to call back."

Dear diary, I saw Mawuli Gavor today and I concluded to myself that I really need Jesus now, more than ever – Heaven is still the goal.

A_Ema

The next story is from the Volume 3 of this book which was written in the year 2000.

50

A Fulfilled Life Without Marriage and/or a Biological Child

I am sick and tired of being sick and tired of the way single ladies do like being single is the worst problem on earth. Other people are going through their own stuff and believe me life's problems are plenty – if you hear other people's woes, you'll just be grateful that the only unanswered prayer you have is marriage.

Life throws a lot of challenges at 99 percent of the human population; it could range from poverty, being in a miserable marriage, not having kids or having a child or two with major health impairments, demonic attacks, not having enough money to feed, having a serious health condition, being a single mum (either widowed, divorced, abandoned or by choice) with children to take care of and not enough money to do that, etc.

In fact, no one should do like their own problems are the worst mbok, everyone is going through, has gone through or will go through their own share of life's ups and downs so being single is just one of them - carry your own.

In addition, whether we like it or not, some people will die without getting their 'important' prayer (s) being answered by God (for whatever reason – will of God, lack of faith or just ignorance).

I'm just from the burial of one of our pastors' wife. She was one woman I respect a lot – in spite of the top position her husband has in one of the leading oil companies, she is really a modest and down to earth person who relates with everyone easily.

She fell in love, got married and after over ten years of being married, died without her own biological children – thank God she and her husband adopted 2 kids. I thank God for her life because though she could not biologically populate the earth, she populated God's kingdom with a lot of souls and brought smiles to a lot of people by helping them get their own biological children.

As I read all the nice things people said about her, I cannot help thinking of Dorcas in the Bible whom Peter raised to life by the power in Jesus' Name because the impoverished cried out for her sake since she had been a source of great blessings to them.

If prayers could solve all problems, I am sure that she would have come back to life too – in the end, we are all subject to God's mercy.

What touched me the most was that she dedicated herself to see that other families that sought the birth of children had theirs in spite of her several failed attempts. I believe the whole experience must have been emotionally, psychologically, financially and spiritually draining for her both at the home front and before the society.

Nevertheless, she still helped others achieve what she could not and desired so much to achieve for herself.

As a pastor's wife, I believe she prayed for others and carried their babies to the altar of God during their naming and child dedication ceremonies, yet she never carried her own biological children. She had the choice to wallow in self-pity, depression and bitterness (against God or whoever).

On the contrary, she took her destiny in her hands and decided that if life gives her lemons, she will make lemonades out of it for people to drink and be blessed. She impacted lives while on earth and even in death her story is transforming lives.

I must appreciate God for the husband she had. I believe his support was the sail beneath her wings. May the Lord bless all supportive husbands.

My point in all this is we should not come and go and come and kill ourselves for things we do not have. We should appreciate God for the things He has blessed us with and make lemonades from our lemons.

With all these, I rest my case. I shall make the best of my life and find joy in all the blessings God has in store for me as I still wait in hope in God for my marriage to take place, and if it doesn't may I not go down in history just as someone who lived her life living only for the hope of getting married.

I will enjoy my life, pursue and get other good things I can get out of life (all that talk about how it is not good for a single lady to look too 'rich' is nonsense, suppose I don't even get married and besides the guy did not come when I was broke). I will reach out to others, find fulfilment in life from my work with God and the children I reach out to, impact lives around me positively, make lemonades from my lemons and enjoy it.

Las las, this whole wanting to get married and have kids, what are the guarantees? People have married early and never had kids and even those that have, what is the guarantee that they will be there for you in your old age – no one knows tomorrow.

The ones that will be there for you by God's grace are those (including your biological children) whose lives you have impacted for good whether you are single or married.

Jesus is what we all need! Heaven and earth are real and it will be disastrously risky if one leaves this earth to discover that eternity in heaven or earth is real and one CANNOT go back to the earth to receive Jesus and follow Him faithfully.

It is better to take the risk to accept Jesus now while one still has the breath of life.

I am glad I have Jesus - He makes all the difference.

A_Ema

There are a lot of loose ends and they will be tied up in the Volume 3

• Will we be having our happy ending with Ema's wedding to Michael (when her heart is beating for Andy)

• What did Sister Cynthia do with her pregnancy (or baby if she didn't abort it?)

• Did Ema attend the school re-union and if she did, did she come out worse or better for it?

For the volume 3, send an email to thesecretdiaryscl@gmail.com, using 'Request for Volume 3' as the subject of the mail.

If you haven't read Volume 1, simply send an email to thesecretdiaryscl@gmail.com, using 'Request for Volume 1' as the subject of the mail.

Alternatively, for any of the volumes, enquiries or for speaking engagements, send a WhatsApp message to 08052574493 (or an email to thesecretdiaryscl@gmail.com).

- Do you want to share your good or bad experiences as a Christian lady?
- Do you want ideas on how a single lady can get married as soon as possible?
- Do you want ideas on how to effectively utilize your 'marriage-waiting' period?
- Do you want to meet with other people going through your experiences or you want professional help?
- Are you a Christian and just want to rant about your experiences without anyone condemning or criticizing you for not being 'strong' in the faith?
- Or perhaps, you just want to gist about issues raised in the stories in this book with other readers.

Then join our blog or Facebook page

Blog - www.secretdiary.net

Facebook – web.facebook.com/groups/thesecretdiaryscl/

For more enquiries, questions, speaking engagements, personal questions or direct questions to Ema, reach us via

Email – thesecretdiaryscl@gmail.com

Mobile – 08052574493 (WhatsApp only)

GLOSSARY

Chapter 27

Abeg - Please

Sef - Anyway

You wey dey get boyfriends – you that get boyfriends regularly

Runs girl – a lady who sleeps with men for money

Shey – making the question a tag question (in this context)

Chei! – An exclamation of sorrow

Abi o!! - Yes o! (in this context)

Chapter 28

Tamuno Imiebam!   – God thank you (in Ibani language – a language from the Ijaw tribe)

Chapter 29

Mbok – please (in Ibibio language)

Chapter 30

No gree me rest o – disturbed my peace

Chapter 31

Wahala no dey end   – problems do not finish

Biko   – please (in Igbo language)

I tire   – I'm tired

Chapter 32

Sha   – anyway

Na   – used for emphasis

Shey   – used to make a question a tag question

Chapter 33

Na wa!   – Exclamation of unhappiness

Na   – too

Hian!!   – Exclamation of shock

Shey I should have been married by now, abi?"   – I guess I would have been married by now, right?

Abi?   – right?

Abeg   – Please

Chapter 34

Mbok, I dey think my life   – Please, I am thinking about my life

She no marry or she marry late, wahala; when she marry, she never born, double wahala; she born sef and she born only girls, make she just prepare herself for another dimension of problem   – If she doesn't get married or gets married late, she'll face problems; when she gets married and hasn't given birth, more trouble; if she gives birth to only girls, she should just prepare herself for another dimensions of problems.

...you no say we no dey tire for prayer for Naija, our problems too much - plus village people   – you know that we don't get tired of prayers in Nigeria, our problems are too much; In addition to witchcraft devices sent against us from relatives in our villages

Chei! & Eh   – exclamation of sadness in this context

Chapter 35

Na dem dey rush us o   – we are in serious demand

Even she sef tire!   – she is also tired

Let him pack well joor!   – he should stay out of her way

Chaiking   – slang for how a guy asks a lady out

Chapter 36

I Don Tire for Near Miss Marriage Proposals! – I am tired of failed marriage proposals

Abeg, I no fit shout – Please, I don't want to shout

Chapter 37

Na wa for you o - How ignorant are you? (in this context)

Chapter 38

That one na husband? - Is that one a husband?

Why you dey like to do like sey na you know too much? Emma, abegi, you too dey do like say na you dey work pass - Why do you like acting like you know too much? Emma, please, you like to do like you are the one that works more than everyone else?

Abeg, I no fit shout! - Please, I cannot shout!

Chapter 39

Shebi... - it makes the question a tag question

Chapter 40

Abi - or (in this context)

How nau? - How are you doing?

Ke - a meaningless sound that is said to demean something or someone

Chapter 41

Na wa for you o! - Are you so ignorant?

Mbok - Please in Ibibio language (a tribe in Nigeria)

Na wa - An exclamation of displeasure

To born pikin - To give birth to a child

Chai! - An exclamation of sadness

Chapter 42

I go dey look like person wey escort others come world - I will like someone who is not doing as well as others

This world I come so - As I was born into the world

Abeg o, I cannot come and go and kill myself - A slang that means one has to take life easy and not beat oneself up because of problems

Oya - Ok

Na Oriental I dey target now - Going to the Oriental Hotel is my next target

Chapter 43

Hian! - An exclamation of disbelief

Man wahala o - Man problems

Chapter 44

I just dey laugh am   - I am just laughing at him

Drink garri   - A special way of eating 'garri' in water

Chapter 45

Pastors wey dey see road anyhow   - Pastors that claim they can see into one's past and future

Chapter 46

I just dey look am   - I am just looking at him

Chapter 47

Something miss am   - She is lucky she escaped

Abi dem send am after me?   - Did evil people/the devil send him against me?

Chapter 48

Darling ke? These men sef, dem too do   - Darling? Some men just like to do too much

...time reach, all of us go show our true self - In time, we will stop the act and be ourselves

Chapter 50

Las las   - In the end.